For Margolee

CHAPTER ONE

It's hard to know where to begin telling you about this. I wonder if there's even such a thing as a beginning—or maybe there is, but you can never pin it to one time or one place. You just stop one day and look around and you're in the middle of it. I guess for some people it's OK not to try to figure out how things turned out the way they did. But I know that if I don't at least try, I'll stay the way I am till it kills me. Till I kill me, I mean. I never really accept that that's what I'm doing—I say it, but I don't believe it.

Things don't happen the way they do in movies, with clear-cut reasons. If my parents had deserted me or beaten me up or if I'd been deprived in some visible way, I could say, "See? *This* is why." Even if it weren't the whole truth, it would look and sound legitimate. But I can't say any of those things. I kind of feel like I'm trying to locate the original melody in a fugue.

Take the fall I changed schools. I was in the middle of it all then, and I didn't even know it.

"Is Cavett your real name?" I said. We were sitting on the bus on the way home from school.

"Unfortunately," she replied. "It was my mom's maiden name."

"You'll probably appreciate it when you're older. Like opera, and fish."

Cavett laughed. "What?"

"Yeah, my mom's always saying, 'You don't know what's good. You'll like it when you're older.'" I paused. "Only I'm fourteen and I still hate opera. And fish."

"They always think they know you better than you do," Cavett said, sighing. "Did they tell you you'd like Barrow, too?" It was Cavett's second year at the Barrow School for girls, and my first.

"Natch," I said, making a face. Actually I'd wanted to go there; I could have gone other places, but they were all enormous and everyone was taking one drug or another, and I was scared. At least at Barrow I felt safe. "We get off here," I said, as we came to Central Park West. "That's where I live." I pointed to an apartment building on the next block, and we walked there in silence.

"Hi, Fred," I said as we entered the lobby. Fred, the doorman, was slumped back in a chair with a shredded *Daily News* balanced precariously on one knee.

"Oh, h'llo there, Leslie," he drawled.

"He's dead drunk," I whispered to Cavett. "Come on." We took the elevator up to nine. "Anybody home?" I yelled when we were inside.

"Hi!" I heard Mom call. "In here."

2

"Hey, Mom, I brought a friend home," I said as we entered the kitchen. Mom looked elated. "Mom, this is Cavett French. She's in my class."

"It's so nice to meet you," she said, wiping her hands on a dish towel and smiling. She shook Cavett's hand.

"It's nice to meet you, too, Mrs. Hiller."

"Cavett's normal, like us," I announced. "Except she lives on the East Side." Cavett laughed.

Mom scowled at me and said to Cavett, "Excuse my daughter. She's too honest." Then she kissed my cheek. "Would you girls like a snack?" Mom said, and without waiting for an answer began going through the refrigerator. "Go on in to Leslie's room, and I'll bring it."

"Come on," I said, and Cavett followed me down the hall and into my room. "That's my cat. Hey, Harry," I said, stooping to scratch his back. He gazed up at me lovingly and nipped my leg. "He only bites people when he's madly in love with them," I explained.

Cavett crouched down and scratched him, then got up and walked to the middle of the room. "Where'd you get this?" she said, fingering a painted eggshell hanging from the overhead lamp.

"I made it. It has the four seasons painted on it, see?" I said, turning it around. "To go with Vivaldi."

"It's beautiful!"

I shrugged as Mom walked in with a tray of cookies and some Cokes.

"What a beautiful egg," she said reverently. I glared at her. "I went to Altman's today," she said quickly, placing the tray on my desk.

3

"Oh, yeah?" I said. "What a morgue. Did you get anything?"

"I got a dress," Mom said mournfully.

"Well, don't sound so happy. Don't you like it?"

Mom shrugged. "Not really. You'll hate it."

"Why'd you buy it?"

"It was on sale." She smiled at me. "But I got you a sweater. Purple."

"*Not* on sale, I suppose," I said quietly, and then forced a smile. "You're impossible."

Mom giggled. "Being stingy is fun! It's like a game."

Cavett was on her third Oreo.

"So." Mom sat down on my bed. "Is Cavett your real name?"

I looked at Cavett and grinned.

"It was my mom's maiden name," she chanted.

"Put in another quarter and she'll say it again."

"Oh, that's *nice*," Mom said, ignoring me. "Do you have any brothers or sisters?"

"I have two sisters. Annie's thirteen, and Lauren's nine."

"Do your sisters go to Barrow, too?"

"Annie does."

They kept chatting as I stood by watching, and when I finally slipped out of the room, they didn't even notice. I wandered into the kitchen and stared out the window at the park, eating a chocolate chip cookie. I feel guilty and I don't know why, I thought. Like I've done something evil. It's been like that ever since I can remember; I'd suddenly be overcome with guilt and could never

4

figure out why. I'm glad Cavett likes Mom. All my friends like her. I'm lucky—hardly anyone I know gets along with their mothers. I wonder when they'll notice I'm gone.

"Leslie! Where are you?" Mom called cheerfully. I looked at my watch; twenty minutes had gone by. I walked slowly down the hall and stood stiffly at the door of my room.

"Cavett, you want to go to the park?"

"Sure," she said, and Mom got up. I picked up the tray, and Mom followed me in to the kitchen.

"She's nice, Leslie," Mom whispered.

"Yeah," I said, pleased in spite of myself. "Isn't she?"

"You have such nice friends."

"She likes you, too."

"Oh," Mom said, flicking her wrist modestly.

"She does, I can tell. All my friends like you." She beamed.

Cavett came and stood expectantly at the kitchen door.

"Let's go," I said jauntily.

"Cavett, would you like to stay for dinner?" Mom said.

"I can't, I have a baby-sitting job at six. But thanks anyway."

"Another time then."

"I won't be late," I called as we went out the door.

We walked for a long time without saying much, which was nice—I can't stand being with people who feel like they have to talk all the time. Finally we got to the sailboat pond and plopped down on a bench.

"You have a brother, right?" Cavett said.

"Yeah, Sammy's eight. And a pain."

"Mm."

"What do your parents do?" I asked.

"My dad's a producer, and my mom's an actress."

"Really? What's she been in?"

"Bit parts, mostly, but she just landed a part in a soap. What about yours?"

"My dad teaches piano at Juilliard, when he's not on concert tours. My mom's in real estate. My brother can't do a damn thing, but he's happy."

"And you paint."

"*And* write, *and* play piano."

"No *ballet!*" she exclaimed in mock horror.

"I put my foot down. I shouldn't have. Then I wouldn't be fat."

Cavett looked me up and down. "You're not fat, you're just right."

I looked at the ground, embarrassed. "I want to lose ten pounds."

"You really don't need to."

"I do," I said stubbornly, and turned away.

"Hey, I saw a letter in your room addressed to Leslie M. Hiller. What's the *M* for?"

"Well . . ." I hesitated. "It's for Margolee."

"Margolee? That's a nice name. I've never heard it before."

"It's after one of my mother's cousins who was killed in a concentration camp."

Cavett's mouth dropped open, and finally she said, "God. That's awful."

"Nearly everyone in her family was killed. You know why that one died?" I turned to look at her. "When they were sending people to the left and to the right, they sent Margolee's mother to the left to be killed because she was old. So Margolee went with her. Otherwise she might be alive." I paused. "Cavett, what would you have done?"

"I don't know," Cavett said slowly. "I think I'd probably have gone to the right . . . I don't know."

I suddenly felt like crying.

"Hey, look—a Good Humor man," Cavett said, jumping up in obvious relief.

"How can you eat so much and stay so thin?" I wailed.

She shrugged. "Don't know. My mom says when I'm older, it'll catch up with me."

"What a future. We'll be fat, fish-eating opera freaks."

Cavett laughed. "Come on." We each got a Toasted Almond and walked east till we came out on Fifth Avenue. Cavett leaned over to look at my watch. "My God, it's ten to six! I've got to go."

"OK. Hey, thanks for coming," I said, feeling shy.

"I had fun! Will you take the bus home? Don't walk through the park."

"Yeah, I'll take the bus, I guess."

"See you in gym tomorrow."

"Don't remind me," I moaned.

Cavett nodded sympathetically, giving me a friendly

punch. "I'll hold your ankles for sit-ups so you can bend your knees, OK?" she called, walking backward across the street.

"You got it!" I waved and went to the bus stop.

There wasn't a bus in sight, so I perched on the stone wall surrounding the apartment building on the corner to wait. Well, I have one friend at school anyway, I thought. And Mom likes her. Mom. Why'd she have to do that with the dress and the sweater? When she gives me things, it hurts. But she can't be hurting me on purpose, so how can I get angry? I don't know, the times I love her most I always feel like crying. I miss her sometimes when I'm in the same room with her! Like I'm not really *with* her. And another thing—I get homesick sometimes, which wouldn't be strange except I'm usually at home when it happens. I've never been able to tell anyone about this—I'm ashamed of it. It would sound so peculiar. I love my father, too, but it's different. He doesn't make me sad. Maybe I love her too much. I don't ever want her to die.

"Sammy, eat your chicken," Mom said.

"I'm full," he whined.

"No wonder you're full, you fill up on potato chips, and then you can't eat your dinner," Dad said, reaching for the broccoli.

"He eats that crap because it's in the house," I said, eyeing Sammy enviously. He was thin as a reed. "If you don't want him to eat it, don't buy it."

8

"Shut up, Leslie," Sammy said cheerfully. "Look, Leslie didn't eat her chicken either."

"I had a Good Humor," I confessed.

"Aha!" Sammy screamed. "And you talk about *me* eating junk!"

"Ice cream, for your information, is not junk. Remember Hilda?"

Dad nodded. Hilda was my German nurse. She took care of me until I was four because Mom had to work full time then. She couldn't speak a word of English, and I was completely bilingual. "No ices—ice *cream*. No orange drink—orange *juice*," I said.

"Hilda gave you nightmares," Sammy said.

"You don't know what you're talking about. You weren't even born," I snapped.

"Mommy told me. She read you scary stories in German, and you had nightmares."

"Oh, go watch TV," I muttered.

"Can I? Can I?" he begged.

"Go, go," Dad said, and Sammy dashed out of the dining room. "So, Leslie, I heard you brought home a friend today." *Gee, Mom, why don't you notify the newspapers?* I thought. I looked at them and felt instantly ashamed. How can I be so mean?

"Yeah, Cavett French."

"Isn't that some name!" Mom said.

"So, Dad, any interesting students this year?" I said, not looking at Mom. Dad's eyes twinkled.

"Nobody you'd be interested in, I'm afraid," he said.

"You don't want a musician," Mom said.

I stared at her. "That's terrible!" I exclaimed.

"I was just kidding," Mom said hastily.

"Well, you better be!" Dad laughed, and began clearing the table.

"Anyway, how do you know what I want?" I persisted.

"I *said* I was kidding," Mom said. No, please, don't let us fight. I don't want to fight. "Leslie, your sweater's in the living room if you want to see it," she called from the kitchen.

"What sweater?" Dad said, following me.

I opened the bag and pulled it out. It was gorgeous— a plum-colored V neck.

"Mom! I love it!" I yelled.

"You really do?" she said, coming in. "Try it on." I obliged. "What a luscious color on you. Max, look at her eyes."

"Hey, blue eyes, you're gorgeous," Dad said. "Did you find anything for yourself, Ruth?"

"A dress. I think I'll try to return it."

"Of course. God forbid you should keep it." Dad sighed. "Hopeless, your mother."

"Oh, shush. Max, don't forget to call Wilfred back. He called you twice." Dad smacked his forehead as he dashed into the piano room, shutting the door behind him.

"He *never* walks, he always *runs*," Mom said affectionately. She settled down on the couch, put on her glasses, and began embroidering. I picked up Harry and sat in the rocking chair, tickling him behind his ears. He began purring loudly, kneading his paws in my stomach.

"Hey, puss," I whispered. "What are you embroidering, Ma?"

"What do you think?"

"Pillows again?" Mom had a thing about pillows. She made things all the time, crocheting and knitting and all that, but pillows were what you could call her biggest export item. "Jesus, where are you going to put them? You put any more on the couch and we won't have room to sit!" I jumped up to tickle her, hanging onto Harry with one arm, and jumped back into the chair. "Mom, do you love me?"

"What a question!" she hooted.

"Do you?"

She put down her embroidery. "I love you more than anything in the world."

"How much do you love me?" It was a game we played when I was little.

"From here to the moon and back again," she answered.

"That's not enough!" I shouted. A curious kind of longing swept through me. Mom, will you always love me to the moon and back? No matter what I do? No matter where I go? But if I don't stick around to hear you tell me, I'll never be sure. "I love *you*, Mom. More than anyone in the whole wide world. More than *anyone*," I repeated.

She looked at me gratefully, but her eyes, as always,

11

looked frightened. "I'm a nag sometimes."

"True. And I'm impossible sometimes. We're still the best."

Later I went to my room and shut the door. Then I tried on the sweater again, examining myself in the full-length mirror. I didn't lie; the sweater *is* gorgeous. Without me under it. I look fat in this, but if I don't wear it, she'll be hurt. And I can't hurt *her*. If only I could lose ten pounds, I thought. Why am I so weak? I wouldn't be half bad-looking if I were thin. 5'5½", blue eyes, long light brown hair, small hips—and 125 pounds. If I were thin, my life would be perfect. It's the only flaw. I turned sideways. Oh, well, I thought. It'll look OK with jeans, I guess. And the pink coral necklace. Passable anyway. I'll get around to being svelte *one* of these days.

"Right, Harry?" I said. He opened one eye, sneered at me, and went back to sleep.

CHAPTER TWO

At first, I really made an effort to make friends at Barrow, but I found that in order to feel as though I belonged, I had to stop being me. Whether or not I was thrilled with who I was was beside the point; it was simply that I didn't feel comfortable being somebody else, not having had any practice at it, and it wasn't a skill I was anxious to acquire. Cavett was really the only friend I had there. There was something terrifically comfortable about being with Cavett—she wasn't anything like the best friends I'd had at my old school. She never read anything unless it was assigned for a class, she had no idea what she wanted to do when she got out of school, and what really impressed me was she wasn't bothered by it in the least. "I'll think of something," she said when I asked her. It wasn't that she was flippant about it, she was just—seriously contented, if that makes any sense.

The other girls at Barrow baffled me. You know that "awkward stage" the lucky ducks like me get to, the one everyone says will pass, no effort involved? Like losing "baby fat"? Well, it seemed the girls at Barrow just skipped it. Just plain skipped right over it, no effort involved. They were graceful and slender—or else they acted as though they were, and so they looked it, too. It's hard to tell the difference sometimes.

In addition to that, I found that at Barrow a C was equivalent to a B or even B+ at my old school. It only took one C on a history paper to get me cracking. I never told Mom and Dad about it. It wasn't that they pressured me about grades, not out loud. But I knew what they expected of me—tops, natch—and no lecture could have had the effect that a look of disappointment on their faces would have had. So I made sure I'd never have to face it.

As I said, the main reason I went to Barrow was to feel safe. The ironic thing, though, was I think I scared the girls in my class. It wasn't anything I *did*, really—I guess that living on the wild and wicked West Side with a musician for a father and wearing lavender knee socks instead of regulation blue was enough. Cavett never seemed to mind things like having to wear a uniform. "It's a lot easier than having to decide what to wear in the morning," she said. Me, I was always wearing *something* that was the wrong color. It wasn't that I resented having rules imposed, even though that's what Cavett thought; I pretended to, but really I enjoyed having rules to break. It was a lot easier not doing what I was supposed to do than trying to figure out what I really wanted. And even when I pretty much *did* know what

I wanted, having a contrast always gave me the certainty I lacked. Some people don't need it, I guess, but for me it really helps.

It's hard to explain because it seemed like I was the opposite of the Barrow girls, who never put up a fight for anything.

But even then, I knew it wasn't true. Like with Mom —we fought over dumb things all the time, but when it came down to important stuff, somehow we always agreed. "You always do the *right* thing," she'd say. She never had to be *ashamed* of me—that's why she loved me, I guess. I was just like her. I couldn't really talk to Cavett about this, even though I could tell her most other stuff. I'm not sure why—I just knew it would sound weird.

Whenever I told anyone at school that Mom and her family had been in concentration camps—I didn't go around announcing it, but when it came up, I didn't try to hide it—they'd become very silent and look at me as if to say, "Why did you have to tell me that?" One time Marla, a small blond pug-nosed creature who blinked constantly because she insisted on wearing contact lenses that didn't fit properly, said, "Gee, Leslie, you really don't *look* Jewish." The worst part of it was that I felt flattered. I could never tell Mom that. I used to tell her everything—and because I knew I would, I tried to keep a clean slate. I've never done anything horrible on the outside, I don't think—but for some reason, just thinking rotten things made me feel as guilty as if I'd really hurt someone. I'd have made a great Catholic.

I don't mean to sound like some docile drip. Like I said, Mom and I fought all the time. Take my room, for instance. You haven't seen chaos till you've seen my room. At least three of my drawers were always open, with clothes hanging out everywhere. There were piles of papers and records all over the rug, and opening my closet was just asking for a concussion. When my desk got really ratty, I began using it as a palette when I painted; only in one corner, and I thought it looked kind of nice, but Mom nearly died when she saw it. I begged her a million times not to touch my stuff because I could never find anything after she'd put things away—but neatening up was like a sickness with her. We had the most unlived-in living room I've ever seen. The kitchen, though, was nice and messy. I guess when you go through the war, you want a cluttered kitchen.

All in all, though, Mom couldn't complain about me. She would always tell me how her friends envied her for having a daughter like me. My flaws paled beside the tribulations faced by her friends, whose kids "never tell them anything." Somehow that seemed far worse than that the kids were getting high, expelled, pregnant, and God knows what else. It was the lack of sharing that got to her. And that was one thing she didn't have to worry about.

"Cavett, will you please come on?" I said impatiently. It was a Friday afternoon in late October, unusually warm for that time of year, and we were walking down Madison to our favorite café for cappuccino. It was one of those white-tiled, plant-filled places with about twenty different kinds of coffee, delicate French pastries, and a different kind of quiche every day. We went there at least once a week, usually on Fridays because school let out early.

"Wait, I can't find my keys," Cavett said, rummaging through her saddlebag. I glanced nervously at the two men leaning languidly against the mailbox on the corner.

"What do you need them *now* for?" I whispered. "Can't you look for them when we get there?"

She looked up at me. "But if I left them in my locker, I have to go *back*."

I covered my eyes with my hand. "Those creeps are going to start bugging us. I just know it." And sure enough, I heard a hiss and then three loud kisses.

"Hey, sweetheart, come home with me."

"Cavett, let's go," I said softly.

She looked over at them, expressionless. "Just ignore them," she said calmly, digging deeper into her bag.

"Look at those pretty little tits," I heard, and then more kissing and hissing.

"Cavett, *please*," I begged, beginning to feel almost desperate. Why did I wear such a clingy sweater? A sweater that shows off my pretty little embarrassing tits?

"I found them!" she announced, waving her keys triumphantly. The men began approaching us, and I took Cavett by the arm and hauled her along till we got to the next block.

"Cavett, why'd you have to do that?" I said, almost wanting to cry.

She looked at my face and laughed. "Why do you get so upset?"

"Why do *I* get upset? Why don't *you* get upset?"

"I don't know. It doesn't seem worth it, I guess," she said.

I looked at her curiously. "Don't you ever worry about stuff?"

"Sure I do," she said. "Sometimes I do. Not as much as you, though, I guess."

Maybe I inherited it, I thought. Mom's always worried about *something*. And when she's not worried, she gets worried about that! I was pretty brave with those guys, come to think of it. Mom would have dissolved on the spot.

Cavett and I sat at our favorite table on the balcony and ordered cappuccinos and one napoleon.

"You're a terrible influence," I said, referring to the napoleon. Cavett was rummaging through her bag again. After pulling out a pair of gym socks, a copy of *Beowulf*, and three empty Chiclet boxes, she finally produced a pen.

"Here," she said, handing it to me. "I wanted to give you this."

"Hey, a rapidograph! Why are you giving it to me?"

"I got it as a present, and I never use it, and I know you like them, so take it. Annie would kill me if she knew. She loves them."

"Then why don't you give it to her?"

"Because I hate her," she said simply.

18

"Oh. Well, thanks!" I said, and tried it on a napkin.

"Sorry if it's clogged."

I looked at her in exasperation. "What are you apologizing for? Jeez. Anyway, I'm a whiz at fixing things." I replaced the cap and clipped it to the pocket of my blazer. "I've never had one before—I use a Speed-Ball."

"Oh," Cavett said, looking disappointed. That's something I can never do—let people see when I'm disappointed or hurt.

"No, you don't understand. These are made in Germany, and my mom drilled it into me not to buy things that are made there."

"*Oh*," she said, nodding. "Hey—listen—if she'll get mad or something—"

"I won't tell her," I cut in, feeling guilty the instant I said it. I looked at Cavett, waiting to see her reaction. She just nodded and looked out the window, and I sat back in relief.

"I can't believe it's nearly November, you know?" she said.

Our cappuccinos and napoleon arrived, with two forks. We ate silently, watching people come in and out, listening to the soft, refined hum of other people's conversations. Madison Avenue matrons toddled in, King Charles Cavalier spaniels in tow, to buy croissants and lace cookies; streamlined women with leathery suntans and huge pink sunglasses holding their hair in place asked what kind of quiche there was that day. The sun gave everything that special glow you see only on October afternoons, when Halloween is just around the corner and the air is so clear that the buildings flash at you like holiday silverware.

Cavett was gazing around dreamily, her mouth covered with whipped cream.

"Hey, Santa Claus," I said, poking her. "You want to go to the Met?"

She looked outside and then back at me. "It's too nice out," she said, which I knew wasn't the real reason— she got bored at museums but didn't want to say so.

"Hey, I know! Let's take the bus down to the zoo and find the carousel."

She perked up slightly. "The carousel? Wow, I haven't been there since I was a little kid."

"Me neither. Come on." I picked up the check before Cavett could begin hunting for her wallet, saying, "My treat. To thank you for the pen. And to get out of here before sundown."

"Ho, ho, ho."

The instant we got to the zoo I was sorry we'd gone, but Cavett didn't seem bothered, and I felt silly turning back. There were hardly any people there—a few scattered bums with matted hair prowling through garbage cans, and a row of old men and women, faces tilted upward, eyes closed, catching the late-afternoon sun. I had this crazy urge to run over and hug them, tell them that even though their kids never called them and they never saw their grandchildren, *I*, Leslie M. Hiller, cared.

"Cavett, look," I said. "Those could be our grandparents." She looked at me blankly. "Cavett—Cavett, that man. He looks like he's dead!" She followed my gaze to a frail, faded man of about eighty, chin resting on his chest, hands frozen in a half clutch in his lap.

"You're right," she whispered, standing stock-still. "God, what do we do if he is?" We crept a few feet closer, staring at him intently. Suddenly his head rose with a start, and his newspaper slipped off his lap onto the pavement.

I straightened up. "He's alive."

"What a relief," she said earnestly, brushing her bangs with the back of her hand and shaking her head. I covered my mouth and began to laugh.

"Come on, this is terrible," I said, thinking that if I weren't laughing, I might burst into ridiculous baby sobs.

We followed the signs pointing to where the carousel was, passing the empty lion and elephant cages, following the narrow hilly paths through the park.

"Look, Wollman's skating rink," I said. "I used to go there every Wednesday."

"Where is this thing anyway?" Cavett said, shading her eyes and peering around like a sailor. "Are you sure we didn't go the wrong way?"

Then I saw it and began to run. When I got to the top of the hill, I stopped.

"It's closed," Cavett said breathlessly when she caught up with me. Of course; it was October. "Can we sit down before we leave?"

We sat on a bench for a few minutes, staring at the small enclosed structure. A brass plaque read: "Michael

Friedman Memorial. This merry-go-round replacing a famous landmark is a gift to the children of the city by the Michael Friedman Foundation 1951."

Cavett rubbed her hands together. "I'm getting cold. Can we go now?"

"Yeah," I said, standing up. "Oh, Cavett—can we please go to your house and watch TV?"

"That's the best idea you've had all day," she said, and we got up and began running.

"Mom?" I yelled as I dropped my jacket on the chair in the foyer. Harry came over and rubbed up against my leg, and I heard Chopin coming out of the piano room. I went to Sammy's room.

"*Heavens*, child, what *are* you doing?" I said sarcastically, looking at the book in his lap.

"Hebrew," he said in a long-suffering voice.

"Mom's always saying you *love* Hebrew."

"I don't. I hate it," he said without much conviction.

"It's OK to like it, you know. Even if she wants you to." He smiled at me, and I sat on the floor and crossed my legs.

"I like it when we talk about history and stuff," he admitted. "But I *don't* like having Hebrew lessons on Wednesdays, which is the one day we get out *early* and all my friends are in the *park*," he said vehemently.

"Yeah, I know what you mean," I said. "Hey, where's Mom?"

"The Russells are having a party tonight, so she's bringing over some dip she made."

22

"Why couldn't she bring it later?"

" 'Cause she and Daddy are going late, and she didn't want them to starve or something," he explained. "You know her."

"Mm," I grunted. "Hey, Sammy. Am I pretty?"

"You're beautiful," he said seriously.

"Come on."

"You are."

"Do you think Cavett is pretty?"

He thought for a moment. "She's *nice*," he said finally.

I looked at him in admiration. I happen to like Cavett's looks. She isn't what you'd call pretty, exactly. She has scruffy reddish hair that never falls in the same direction, so it looks like she put on curlers zigzagged instead of in rows. Her face is sort of ordinary, except for her eyes, which are perfectly round, like two brown M & M's, and always look slightly bewildered. But I knew what Sammy meant.

"You're a good kid. Anyone ever tell you that?" I said.

"Yeah, I'm not bad," he said, shrugging sheepishly.

"Well." I stood up and stamped my foot, which had fallen asleep. Dad was still playing, but in our house music was like traffic—you just don't hear it after a while. Then a melody began to register.

"Hey!" I said, and hopped out and down the hall to Dad's piano room. I opened the door quietly and crept in. Dad was like a bat—he played in the dark. The room faced south, not east, so the sunlight was blocked by the adjacent apartment building, and still, he kept the shades down. I sat on the small velvet sofa, and he stopped playing and looked over at me.

"Can I listen? You're playing my mazurka."

He looked so pleased I felt awful—as if it was a surprise to him that I wanted to hear him play. "I'd love nothing more," he said grandly. And he played it for me from the beginning.

It's a fairly short piece, but you get completely swept away by it. He played it as though he were riding big, wonderful waves, and it made me feel like leaping around a Viennese ballroom like an idiot. Free, that's how it made me feel. Free and unself-conscious and beautiful. That might sound dumb, but I can't help it, it's the truth.

"That was great," I said with gusto when he'd finished, afraid of letting him see how I felt.

"Am I still better than Horowitz?" he joked.

"No, not Horowitz. Rubinstein," I corrected. "Horowitz plays in black and white. Rubinstein plays in color."

He laughed. "What do I play in?"

"You play in color, too, but better." I heard the door creak slightly and turned to see Mom peeping in.

"Am I interrupting something?" she said.

"I've been giving a concert for my harshest critic, and she approves," Dad said. "And now, if you'll excuse me, ladies I have to get back to work."

"OK," I said, getting up.

"But you're welcome to stay."

"No, it's OK," I said a little reluctantly, looking at Mom's retreating figure. "I'll help Mommy with dinner."

24

I stalled in the living room, wandering over to the blond cabinet along the far wall and fingering the knick-knacks collected over the years: two glass birds from Sweden; a wooden angel painted candy pink and yellow with one wing missing; a seashell I'd decorated with sequins and beads in kindergarten; a black lacquered box from the Far East, red on the inside, which smelled like ammonia when you opened it; three little iron soldiers; an olive-wood camel from Israel that Harry had teethed on; a bell from Ceylon. Darkness had come without my noticing. I rubbed my eyes in the half-light and, feeling suddenly lonely, hurried into the kitchen, where Mom was stirring something in a huge pot.

"Mmmm," I said, taking a deep breath and sitting down at the table. "What's in the caldron?"

"Veal stew. You'll have to feed yourself and Sammy. Daddy and I are going to the Russells, OK?"

"Fine. When will it be ready?"

"I'd say in another hour," she said, poking at the contents with a fork and withdrawing her hand quickly as the steam penetrated.

"Hey, Mom? What happened to your arm?" I said, looking at the small round Band-Aid inside her elbow.

"I went for a blood test today," she said, sprinkling some oregano into the pot.

"Why? What's wrong?"

"Nothing. I've just been feeling a little tired lately. It's nothing."

"What kind of test are they doing then?"

"Just to see if I'm still anemic. I'm sure I'm fine."

"Well, *good*," I said in exasperation. "But weren't you taking pills or something?"

"Well, yes, but I stopped. Leslie, there's ice cream in the freezer for dessert."

"Did the doctor say you didn't need the pills anymore?" I pressed.

"Oh, they're all in cahoots with the pharmacists," she said, waving her hand in annoyance.

"Mother," I said plaintively, "do you do this to torture me?"

She laughed. "Of course, why else? Every night before I go to bed, I say to myself, 'Now how can I torture Leslie?'" She glanced up at the clock. "Oh, Jesus, I still have to shave my legs!"

"Wear pants," I suggested pointlessly, since Mom never wore pants when she went out. "Hey, guess where I went today. The carousel."

"In Central Park?" she said, lowering the flame and running out of the kitchen. "Max! Get dressed!" she shrieked. I followed her and stood at the bathroom door. "I'm sorry. You went to the carousel," she repeated. "Did you have fun?"

"Not really," I said distractedly, almost wishing I hadn't told her.

"No? . . . Oh, Leslie, Robin called you. I told her you'd call her back. You never see her anymore," she said, looking at me hopefully. "Why don't you invite her for dinner tomorrow? I'll make eggplant."

"Maybe," I said, feeling angry without knowing why. I know, it must be just that I'm a normal fourteen-year-old, I told myself sensibly. I'm supposed to be moody and difficult, right?

"Don't forget to call her back, or she'll think I didn't give you the message."

"I will, I will," I said, going to my room and shutting the door behind me. Robin had been my best friend at my old school. Unlike Cavett, she was a voracious reader, slightly overweight and bold, which I loved. Once, when we were twelve, we went to the Russian Tea Room for coffee, dressed like absolute slobs, and when we sat down Robin reached into her knapsack and whipped out a ham sandwich and began eating it. I still can't believe we got away with it without getting kicked out; I guess the manager thought it'd be easier to let it go than to make a scene. Mom told that story to so many people I began wondering who got more of a bang out of it, her or me. I guess it shouldn't have mattered, but telling myself that never seemed to do much good.

Anyway, when I went to Barrow, Robin went to Stuyvesant, and even the few times I'd spoken to her since September I noticed a change in her. She had a group of new friends and always seemed to be going places with them, like parties and stuff, which is something completely foreign to me. At our school no one ever had parties, or if they did, it was all-girls and we went to plays or movies. The way Robin described the parties she went to, I couldn't imagine anything more depressing. Why would anyone want to sit around in the dark listening to loud music, necking with some slobbery, sweaty guy you hardly even know?

I decided I'd call her anyway, though—she called *me*, so maybe she's still the same, and I just haven't talked to her enough to know it.

CHAPTER THREE

I t turned out Robin had called to invite me to go to a Halloween parade with her and a bunch of her friends. I'd never heard of it before, but apparently every Halloween there's this parade in Greenwich Village. A friend of hers, Marilyn Somebody, had discovered it by accident the year before. Marilyn was in some Greek place on Halloween eating felafel when she started seeing people dressed in incredible costumes pass by, one after another, all heading the same way. So she dropped her felafel and ran after them to see what it was. The parade started in the West Village and picked people up along the way, and they were dressed in elaborate, professionally made costumes—dragons, skeletons, you name it; even a whole troupe of men dressed as giant Crayola crayons. There were people swallowing swords and fire and doing magic tricks and playing eerie music on medieval instruments.

"It sounds like a Breughel painting, you know?" Robin said. "And Marilyn says everyone comes out on the balconies to watch, and there are jack-o'-lanterns in all the windows, *and*—get this—there's a stuffed devil with a spotlight on him on top of the arch in Washington Square Park, and at midnight they throw him off!"

"*Wow.*" It really did sound fabulous. "And your mom won't mind your being out that late?"

"Well, I haven't told her, exactly," she said, giggling.

I told her I couldn't go. I'd promised Cavett weeks before that I'd go to a dance at Horace Mann with her, and frankly I was relieved to have a legitimate excuse. I know I'd have felt funny being with a bunch of kids who all knew each other, and besides, Mom would have been a nervous wreck, and lying to her was out of the question. In our family it was practically a law that whenever anyone went out, they always left a number where they could be reached. Dad started that because he travels so much. I don't think he meant to be morbid, but whenever any of us went anyplace, it was with the knowledge that you-never-know dot-dot-dot. I guess it's the truth, but it's kind of an awful way to live.

Anyway, I probably could have told Cavett I couldn't make it, but I'd have felt lousy. Neither one of us was dying to go to that dance, but her parents were going to a party some producer friend of theirs was having, and Annie had seized the opportunity to throw one of her own. Cavett didn't want to be there, and I didn't blame her. Looking at Annie and Cavett together, you'd never believe they were related. Annie was dark, sultry, almost exotic-looking with long black hair and a deep voice which she kept down to a prank-phone-call whisper. She rarely smiled, went to a cloisonné class once a week, and had a sullen look about her that seemed to drive men crazy—at least that's what Cavett told me, and I believe it.

"She makes me feel like some dumb little kid," Cavett told me. "She's a year younger than me, and she's going out with an *eighteen-year-old.*"

"God. What do they do together?" I said.

"I don't know," Cavett said, shaking her head.

"We sound like two little old ladies." Cavett looked at me sadly and smiled. "Cheer up. We'll go to the dance and meet some nice violinists or something, OK?"

The Horace Mann School is in Riverdale, so they'd arranged for a school bus to stop at various points in Manhattan and pick up girls from Barrow, Nightingale, and Chapin. Cavett and I were dressed similarly in jeans, sweaters, and blazers, and we sat in the back of the bus, away from the other Barrow girls, who were clustered up front.

"Look what I got," Cavett said, taking a little blue case out of her shoulder bag. It said "Estée Lauder" on the front. She opened it, revealing two shades of lavender eye shadow.

"You *bought* it?" I said.

"Are you kidding? I found it in Annie's bathroom. She'll never miss it, she's got a million of them. Try some on."

"Me?" I laughed. "I don't know how to put on makeup."

"What's there to know?"

I shrugged, then held it up so I could see my eyes in the little mirror and began brushing some on my left eyelid. "This bus is so bumpy," I said in exasperation, then stopped and blinked at her. "How does it look?"

"Do the other one," she said, and I did. "Hey, you look good!"

"You sure I don't look like someone beat me up?" I said, pleased. I've always been fanatically antimakeup. Mom never wears any either, except when she goes out, she puts on red lipstick. Red lipstick and Ma Griffe cologne. That's all she needs. And she's beautiful. But I'm not a European beauty, I thought, glancing once more into the tiny mirror. I'm a potato-face. A potato-face with lavender eye shadow. Maybe it'll help.

The first half of the dance was predictably depressing. The place was dark and absolutely enormous, decorated with orange and black streamers, and there was a long table in back with bowls of punch, potato chips, and candy. Cavett and I bumped into each other there at regular intervals after braving it around the dance floor separately, trying to look aloof but probably looking terrified, if her face was anything to go by. The band was so loud you couldn't tell if they were good or terrible, which I guess was the point. Marla and her bunch were there, and by nine thirty all of them were dancing.

"Look at them," I said to Cavett during one of our potato-chip encounters. "I don't think those guys have said a word to them all night."

"*What?* I can't hear you!" Cavett shouted above the din.

"That's what I mean!" I shouted back. "How can anyone talk to each other in here? This is worse than the subway!"

"It's better this way," Cavett yelled just as the band stopped for a break. "It's better this way," she repeated in a normal voice. "If they're anything like Annie's friends."

"Airheads. Here we are, two scintillating, fantastic creatures, totally overlooked. It's a crime."

Just then a boy strode over to the table and stopped directly across from me. He was very short, maybe five feet one, with short curly black hair and very pale skin, wearing dark slacks and a light blue button-down shirt.

"Hello," he said in a surprisingly low voice, looking up at me.

"Hi," I replied awkwardly.

"My name is Avram Werner. What's yours?"

"Leslie. Hiller," I added. Now what? I wondered as the band began making noise again.

"Would you like to dance?" he said, leaning across the table so I could hear him.

"Sure," I said, giving Cavett a quick look of disbelief and walking around the table.

"I'm not very good at this," he said as we started dancing.

"Me neither." I looked down at the collar of his shirt. The top button was missing, so I could see his undershirt. There was something endearing about it—it reminded me of Dad. I smiled at him.

"What grade are you in?" he yelled.

"Ninth."

"Me too." We danced then without talking, until the band switched to a slow song. I stood in front of him feeling like a hippopotamus.

"Would you like to go out for a little walk on the quad?" he said, tugging at his collar. "It's very warm in here."

I cased him quickly, decided I couldn't be safer with my own grandfather, and nodded affably.

"I don't like these things very much," Avram said when we were outside. "I'm excellent at waltzing." I raised my eyebrows. "Look!" he cried suddenly. "There's Pegasus!"

"Where?"

"There, see?" He pointed up at the stars. "And there's Andromeda, see? Pegasus and Andromeda meet at Alpheratz. Do you like astronomy?"

"I like stars," I said meekly. "I don't know much about astronomy, though."

"I think I'd like to be an astronomer. But I also enjoy stage direction. We're doing *Carousel* at school this year, and I'm the director." He rambled on about himself, and I listened, amazed. I can't believe it, I thought. He's two feet tall, and he asked me to dance. He's not even worried that I might be bored or think he's weird. I mean I don't, but most people probably would. I just can't believe it.

"Do you play any instruments?" he was saying.

"Piano. My father's a pianist," I said.

"I play the violin," he said, and I burst out laughing. He cocked his head. "Did I say something funny?" I told him what I'd said to Cavett, and he nodded seriously. "It's difficult to find people to talk to. But I like you."

Big wow, I thought, and then looked at him. He smiled so sweetly I couldn't help smiling back. Mom won't believe this, I thought. He's too much.

"So, are you going to be a musician, too?" he asked.

"No. I hate to practice. I guess that means I don't really want to be one. I paint, though, and I make things."

"Really? I'd like to see them sometime."

I felt myself blushing. "I'm not that good."

"You shouldn't put yourself down," he said firmly.

"Oh, I'm not," I said quickly. "I just can't say what I really feel with painting. It's like—with music, I'm re-creating, and with painting, it's just not *enough*." I began to shiver, and he touched my arm lightly.

"You're cold. Let's go back inside."

We didn't dance anymore, and I was kind of sorry. After about fifteen minutes of sitting on the side, I spotted Cavett. I looked at my watch and said, "I think our bus is leaving soon."

"Shall I wait with you?" he said formally.

"No, uh, I see my friend over there. I think I better go before she gets lost and misses it. She's kind of dis-combobulated."

35

"Well." He cleared his throat. "I'm glad I met you, Leslie."

"Me too."

He stood up, and I stalled for a moment, glad for the chance to look up at *him*.

"Can I call you?" he said.

"Um, sure," I mumbled.

He stooped down to pick up a napkin off the floor. "I thought I had a pen," he said, patting his pockets desperately.

I saw a group of girls beginning to leave, and I began backing away. "It's listed," I said. "My father's name is Max. On Central Park West."

"Max Hiller on Central Park West. I'll remember," he said, waving at me.

I got home at a quarter to twelve. Dad was away, and I found Mom sitting on her bed, talking on the phone.

"Hold on, Leslie just walked in," she said as soon as she saw me. "How was it? Did you have a nice time?"

"I met a boy," I said, grinning.

"Really?" she said, giggling like a schoolgirl. "She met a boy," she said into the receiver.

"Is that Judy?"

She nodded. Judy was her oldest friend; they gabbed for about an hour every night on the phone. "What's his name?"

"Avram Werner."

"*Avram?*" she squealed. "That's adorable! What does he look like?"

"He looks like a Munchkin. But he has a cute face, and he plays the violin, and he wants to be an astronomer—"

"Wait!" she shrieked happily, eyes sparkling with pleasure. "She says . . ." she began saying to Judy, then held the receiver out to me. "Judy's dying to hear."

I took the receiver from her. "Judy?" I said, caught up in Mom's excitement. "I couldn't believe it. Most of the guys there were such creeps, but . . ."

I spilled it all out, bubbles and all, with Mom sitting there, eating up every word. And the strangest feeling came over me as I talked—as though I were a float in Macy's Thanksgiving Day Parade and someone had poked a hole in me. The more I told Mom and Judy, the emptier I felt. Mom's enjoying this so much I don't know who went to the dance anymore. Then I thought: It's immaterial. I, Leslie M. Hiller, went to the dance like an empty box. Avram opened it, put a present inside, and I came home all full and gift-wrapped. Mom untied the ribbons, tore off the paper, and took out the gift. Took it away. "I enjoy giving presents so much more than receiving them, Leslie," Mom always says when she gives me things. I'm trying to be like you, Mom. I'm trying so hard—

I gave the telephone receiver back to her, went to my room, and slowly began to undress. I have the best mother in the world, I thought. Nobody could ask for a better mother. She cares, she's interested, she approves . . . but why do I feel so sad? I ought to be happy that she had such a great time at the dance. Does she love me now, more than ever?

When I was in my nightgown, I went back out. Mom had just hung up.

"So tell me more," she said.

There's nothing more to tell. Oh, wait—"He said he'd call me."

"Avram . . . what's his last name again?"

"Werner. Mom, he's so *short*."

"So what? He'll grow."

So what. So what that I feel funny because he's so short. So what that *I* feel *anything*. But . . . but doesn't it matter whether I'm attracted to him or not? I thought it was supposed to matter . . . in some way . . . that it was supposed to matter how I felt about a boy physically. You don't want me to feel those kinds of things, though, do you, Mom? That's why you're so crazy about Avram, the Munchkin. My mind went back to a night the summer I was twelve—the night Roger kissed me. Roger was fifteen, and he lived about a mile from where our house is in Brewster. I hardly knew him. He wasn't very bright, but he was absolutely gorgeous, and when he kissed me, I felt things I'd never felt before. Strange, wonderful things. Almost as though I were flying. When I told Mom about it afterward, a strange look came across her face—embarrassment, partly, but it was more than that.

"That's nice, Leslie," she'd said in a peculiar, distant tone of voice, one I'd never heard before. "But remember—save it."

"Save it?" I'd repeated, puzzled. "For what?"

"For someone you really care about."

I avoided Roger for the rest of that summer and the following summer, when we went back, I found out his family had moved to Maine.

"Did Cavett meet anyone?" Mom said, breaking into my reverie.

"No."

"She will," Mom said reassuringly.

"*Mom*," I said, then stopped myself. Why spoil her fun? "I guess I'll go to bed."

"Sleep tight," she said, kissing my cheek. "I'm so glad you had a nice time!"

I went into my room, shut the door, and sat on the radiator, looking out at the park and wrapping my arms around my legs. There's the Milky Way, and there's the Big Dipper, and . . . and if I open the window all the way and wait long enough, Peter Pan will fly in and take me away, I thought. Every year, when I was little, I watched *Peter Pan* with Liza Bigelow because Liza's parents didn't believe in having a television set. So when *Peter Pan* was on, she slept over, and we watched it together in Mom and Dad's bedroom. If Dad was away, we'd sleep in their bed after it was over, and I'd make Mom open the window all the way. It was almost summertime, always, and I'd lie awake, staring at the stars, waiting.

Peter will fly in, and I can be his mother and pick up his shadow and sew it back onto him . . . but how can you see a shadow if it's sewn on . . . and he'll teach me to fly . . . but Peter doesn't have a mother .

can you fly if you do have a mother?

It was Liza Bigelow who first told me about men and women and the things they do together. It sounded so outrageous to me I told her she must have gotten it wrong, but she said she'd watched her parents do it twice. Mom and Dad never shut their bedroom door all the way, and I only started to when I was eleven or so. Did I ever hear any noise? I don't remember. I don't remember at all. I never asked Mom about what Liza had said —clearly I wasn't supposed to know, or she'd have told me—and then there was fifth-grade science class. Good old Mr. Finkelstein and his gerbils. Liza was right after all.

I heard a soft tapping at the door.

"Leslie? Don't stay up too late."

"I won't," I answered. I waited a minute or so, then went to the mirror and lifted my nightgown.

"Look at that," I whispered. Fat. How can anyone deny it? No wonder the only guy who pays attention to me is a violin-playing Napoleon, I thought. But I wanted a violinist. I mean I wanted someone *intellectual*; then why do I feel so . . . so . . . what *do* I feel? I thought, thoroughly confused. Empty—more than empty. I feel robbed. Tonight isn't mine anymore. It didn't happen to me. It started out being mine, but now it doesn't seem to matter anymore. I should have stuck with Cavett; I shouldn't have abandoned her. Better yet, I shouldn't have gone at all.

CHAPTER FOUR

Something happened to me that night. I still don't know how to explain it. I began waiting; I didn't know what for. As though there were something I'd been wanting for a long time, hadn't thought about very much, and suddenly it began to press at me. I didn't understand it, so what was there to do but wait?

November came and went, and Avram called twice. Mom couldn't understand why I wouldn't go out with him. I wasn't sure myself; I just knew I didn't want to. I sketched the intricate patterns the trees made against the winter sky with my rapidograph and bought hot chestnuts to put in my mittens when my hands became numb. Annie got caught smoking in the bathroom at school; Hanukkah came, and Sammy and I got presents every night. Mom won't be outdone no matter what.

"You're lucky," Cavett said when I told her.

"Yeah," I agreed, knowing I could never make her understand.

And then, right in time for Christmas break, I caught

the flu. That's how I lost the first few pounds—by accident. I didn't even realize I'd lost any weight till the first day I was well enough to go out. I put on my jeans and, after staring in the mirror for a moment, dashed out of my room.

"Look!" I said to Mom ecstatically, sticking both hands inside the waist.

"Oh, *my*," Mom exclaimed satisfactorily. "I'll have to take them in for you."

"I'm going on a diet."

"Good," Mom said absently. Of course, she doesn't believe me, I thought. Why should she? How many diets have I gone on and broken within an hour?

But I knew. For the first time in my life, I felt in control. And I knew I wouldn't break. It was like something in me had finally erupted, you know? Having lost those first few pounds was all the incentive I needed; it would be unforgivable to let this free ride pass, I thought. I can do it this time; I *will* do it. They don't believe me, but they'll see—I'm going to be thin. And happy.

And so it began. I bought every calorie counter on the market, read them cover to cover, reread them. I bought a food scale. I began doing sit-ups. I started out doing 45 a day, and gradually upped the number by nines, till I was doing 675. Nine had been my lucky number since I was seven and told Mom I didn't like it, because the word "nine" reminded me of the word "mean." She said how could I not like nine, it was half of eighteen, which in Hebrew is *chai* and also means "good luck"? So ever since then, nine was my magic number.

42

I always exercised to music; I became a slave to the rhythm of every record I put on. I had put myself on a diet which consisted of three ounces of cottage cheese for breakfast and a minute steak and an apple for dinner. Mom was being very good about it; when she and Dad realized I meant business, they were very respectful. "Such willpower," Dad would say.

For the first month I had dinner at five in the kitchen because by then I was so famished I couldn't last till dinnertime, and since I never ate what everyone else did anyway, it didn't seem to matter. Mom kept me company while I ate. I was going about the whole thing with a kind of frenzy that seemed to frighten her, and when she did fret aloud about my not being properly nourished, I became so enraged that she shut up immediately, looking utterly terrified. Certainly she had no grounds for worrying that I'd starve to death. "Look at these reserves," I'd tell her, pointing at my stomach in disgust. "I could live on myself for months."

You can learn to love anything, I think, if you need to badly enough. I trained myself to enjoy feeling hungry. If my stomach contracts, or I wake up feeling nauseated, or I'm light-headed, or I have a hunger headache, or better yet, all of the above, it means I'm getting thinner. So it feels good. I feel strong, on top of myself. In control. Thanks to the dictator.

The dictator. He/she/it—I've never been sure which —was responsible for my sticking to my regimen. This is going to sound pretty crackers, but it was as though this person, this dictator, had taken up residence inside

43

me to keep me in line. It wasn't simply that I *chose* not to eat; I was forbidden to. Even thinking about eating forbidden foods brought punishment. It's so hard to explain. It was like an iron wall would drop, barring me from even looking and smashing me for trying. "How *dare* you," this voice inside me would say. "You greedy pig!" And I was grateful to have someone looking out for me—a kind of savior keeping me from being weak, and fat, keeping me from hurting. Making me respect myself. Hunger, I thought, is a minuscule price to pay. To be thin, no price is too high. The sky's the limit.

I know I probably sound weird, telling you these things. It's not like I "heard voices" the way you hear them on the radio—not like that. It was like hearing myself think, the way everybody does, I guess—the difference being that it didn't seem to be me doing the talking. Not any part of me I'd never encountered before, anyway. Sometimes I even felt I was cheating when people praised me for my willpower; they don't know I have a little dictator inside forcing me, I'd think. And telling anyone might interfere. So shut up, Hiller. Just shut up and follow the rules.

"And she did, clippety-clop," as they say in storybooks. And people noticed. People at school told me how great I looked; Dad told me how great I looked; even Mom, guardedly, told me how great I looked.

One Saturday in early February Judy was over, and I heard Mom telling her she was worried about my dieting.

"Oh, stop being a Jewish mother," Judy replied. "She's

44

the most well-adjusted kid I've ever met. Leave her alone."

I walked into the living room, bowed ceremoniously, and said, "Thank you, Judith." I turned to Mom, said, "*See?*" and trotted off to the kitchen.

There was a box of marzipan on the table, open. My mouth began to water. I'd become laxer with myself, adding a yogurt or two to my daily rations, and once in a while some dried apricots; but bread, junk food, candy, all the things I loved, were absolutely off limits. Period. I turned away, then turned back. Come on, Leslie, I said to myself soothingly. You're 112 pounds. Only seven more pounds to reach perfection . . . you deserve a little reward. Just one, one little reward. What's all this work for if there's no prize at the end? I gingerly picked out a marzipan strawberry and popped it in my mouth. You know that commercial "You can't eat just one"? I should have known.

Panic-stricken, I began pacing the kitchen like a caged animal. Now you've done it, Hiller. You've ruined it—ruined it—ruined it! You've broken your hold. Bad enough, isn't it, to OD on cottage cheese or apricots, but this—this! *Candy!* Yes, all the ridiculous melodrama of an opera, but this is no stage. This is real. Now you'll never stop, now it's in you, and you'll never make it right again; you'll ruin everything you've worked for. Fat. You'll probably be 117 pounds by tomorrow—right this very second you're gaining weight . . . there must be a way to undo this, there *must* be. I began to sweat. Mom came in to refill Judy's coffee cup.

"Aren't you going to the movies with Cavett?" she said, her back to me.

"Later," I said abruptly, and when she turned to look at me, a strange smile flashed across my face. Mom, Mom, Mom, someone is beating me to death, and you can't see a thing, can you? I wish you could make it stop—don't you come near me. Don't touch me. Out. Get out. I'm full. Smile, smile, smile, Leslie.

What am I going to do? I thought hysterically after she'd gone. Now, then, Leslie, let's go about this logically. When food is inside you, is that *it?* No way of removing it? Your stomach is a land of no return, unless . . . hey. Hey! Wait a minute. How can I be so *dumb?* How did I lose weight when I had the flu?

I walked calmly back through the living room, then dashed into the bathroom and locked the door. I lifted the toilet seat and leaned over. Remember, Leslie, how when Dr. Polaski puts a depressor in your mouth to see your tonsils, you gag? Well, come on, honeybunch, go to it, put your finger in.

At first I pulled it out as soon as I began gagging, but the dictator hammered at me: "This simply won't do, Hiller. Leave it in, jerk, how do you expect it to work otherwise?" And out came the marzipan, not tasting a whole lot different from the way it had on the way in.

I washed my hands and face, feeling as though I'd stumbled upon a miracle. Why didn't I ever think of this before? I wondered. This is the answer. This is like

46

magic! I've undone it—removed the stain, erased the marzipan mistake. And it even tasted good, I thought, laughing at myself in relief. "Double your pleasure, double your fun . . ."

Now I can be a good girl again and get Dad off my back, I thought. He'd been hounding me to start "eating normal food again with the family, like a normal human being." I'd begun to comply by having dinner with everyone else, eating only a small portion of whatever Mom had cooked. Remove the skin from the chicken, and it's even lower in calories than steak; scrape the bread crumbs off the schnitzel; have the fish broiled instead of fried. Casserole, forget it. No way could I fish out all the noodles. So Mom made me a minute steak. I was steadfast; I won.

Now, though, in case of error or weakness, I have a way out. A trick, a trick, a magic trick, I sang silently. I can always throw it up. Have my cake and eat it, too, as it were.

"What're you doing?" I said as I got to my locker. Cavett was sitting on the floor, pen in her mouth, with an open book balanced on one knee and a notebook on the other.

"I'm trying to write this stupid essay for English," she muttered, closing the book and dropping it on the floor beside her.

"What do you have to do?" I said. We were in different English classes, so I could help her with writing assignments. Cavett hated having to write.

"Write an essay on this Emily Dickinson poem," she moaned.

"When's it due?"

"Tomorrow."

"Listen, I'm going to the gym to jog for a while now, but let's go to the café after school and I'll help you, OK?"

She smiled up at me gratefully. "Thanks, Leslie."

I took off my skirt and put on my gym shorts.

"Leslie, you're going to lose those on the first lap," she said.

"I know. I took them in once already, but . . ." I shrugged. "I guess I should find a safety pin, huh?"

"Boy, you're so thin. You're really something, you know? I'd never have that much willpower . . . uh-oh."

"What's wrong?"

"Leslie, you wouldn't happen to have a Tampax on you, would you?"

"Sure. In my locker." I opened it and dug around for a minute, finally producing an unopened box of ten. "Take them all."

"I only need one or two," she said.

"Then keep them for a rainy, ha-ha, day," I said, tossing the box to her. "I haven't had my period since November."

"Good grief," she said, looking aghast. "What's wrong with you?—don't tell me. Avram." We both laughed wickedly.

"*Right*, French, he screwed my kneecap."

"No, really, Leslie," she said seriously. "I mean, shouldn't you see a doctor?"

"I did. My mom took me to her gynecologist."

"And?"

I shrugged. "He said there's nothing wrong with me, and if I wanted, he could give me some pills to induce it, but I said no. I mean what the hell, right? It'll turn up. . . . Hey, I've gotta go. I've only got twenty minutes. Meet me here at three-fifteen," I called as I ran out.

"Let me read the poem," I said after Cavett and I had gotten our coffee. Cavett handed me the open book.

"God gave a loaf to every bird,
    But just a crumb to me;
    I dare not eat it, though I starve—
    My poignant luxury
    To own it, touch it, prove the feat
    That made the pellet mine,
    Too happy in my sparrow chance
    For ample coveting.

It might be famine all around
    I could not miss an ear,
    Such plenty smiles upon my board,
    My garner shows so fair.
    I wonder how the rich may feel,
    An Indiaman—an Earl?
    I deem that I with but a crumb
    Am sovereign of them all."

I read it again, astonished. "Cavett, don't you see what she's saying?"

"Something about being happy with what you've got?" she said haltingly.

"Well—" I looked at it again. "Cavett, I mean, maybe she wasn't being literal, but like—I mean, this is how *I* feel."

"Huh?"

" 'God gave . . . just a crumb to me,' 'I dare not eat it, though I starve'—Don't you see? It's that the feeling she got from starving was *more* than . . . than —listen to the last two lines, Cavett—'I deem that I with but a crumb/Am sovereign of them all.' "

"Leslie, Emily Dickinson wasn't writing the Weight Watcher's national anthem," Cavett said.

"How do you know? I mean, how do you know that she didn't mean it literally?" I said, lost in my own thoughts. I looked at Cavett as she reread the poem, feeling a million miles away. "I guess—you could write about it like—I don't know, say something about her appreciating the little things . . ." I can't help her with this, I thought. Either Cavett is hopeless, or I'm beginning to see things cockeyed. "I'm sorry," I apologized.

"Ah, it's OK, I'll figure out something," Cavett said. "Thanks anyway, though. Maybe you're right. I mean I don't know about stuff like this, you do. You're probably right." She took a big bite of the éclair she'd ordered. "How can you watch me?" she said after she'd swallowed. "Doesn't it bother you?"

50 .

"No, why should it?" I said lightly. "As long as it doesn't bother *you*—" She shook her head no. "Oh, well, don't worry about me. I'm used to it." What a trooper I am. I'm not even lying to Cavett. Sometimes I enjoyed watching people eat—I don't know why. Maybe it's like when Mom enjoys things that I do—even more than me, it seems. The old "I'm so happy for you." *For* you. *Instead* of you. It's very useful when you're dieting. God gave an éclair to every Cavett, but just black coffee to me, I thought.

"Hey, when you go off this thing, don't forget, we're celebrating," Cavett said. "A hot butterscotch sundae at Serendipity's."

"When I'm thin enough."

Cavett shook her head. "Jeez, Leslie, you're thinner than I am!"

I scowled at her. "Don't be ridiculous. You're much thinner than me."

"I am not! I weigh 113 pounds."

"Well, then, you've just got heavier bones or something," I said, dismissing it. "*You're* thin. *I'm* not. But I will be."

111, 110, 109, tick, tick, tick. I threw up whenever I had to. Mom and Dad never knew. It took three fingers down my throat by then, but if it had taken a broomstick, I'd have used that. It was only a last resort; I didn't eat and *plan* on throwing up. It was Mom's dinners that got me. They nagged, and I gave in, half glad. Then I'd excuse myself, go to the bathroom, puke, come back to the table, pleased as punch, saying, "What's for dessert?" They knew I was kidding, but they stopped bugging me. They didn't notice I was getting any thinner—I wore baggy jeans and one of Dad's old shirts around the house anyway, so who could tell what I looked like? I'm nearly there—105, my goal. Incredible. Any day now, I'll be thin.

CHAPTER FIVE

G o on, have a chocolate," Dad said, holding the
box out to me.

"No, I don't want one," I lied.

"Come on, just one," he coaxed as Mom came in
from the kitchen and sat down with us in the living
room.

"Hey—I know," I said. "I can chew it and spit it out."

Mom looked up at me sharply. "No. Either you eat it,
or you don't."

"Come on, Ruth, if it gives her pleasure, why shouldn't
she?" Dad said, and I jumped up to go to the kitchen,
returning with a napkin.

". . . not right, there's something not right," Mom
was saying as I entered.

I picked out two and chewed each one, spitting them
both out into the napkin. Sammy was standing in the
doorway, watching.

"What's she doing?" he yelped.

"Spitting out chocolate, creep," I said.

53

"Gross! That is so gross," he said.

"Shove it!"

"Leslie!" Mom said.

"Go sit on a pencil and rotate," Sammy said to me, ignoring her.

"Sammy, Jesus, where did you hear that?" Mom screeched, blushing.

"At school," he replied coolly, the chocolate forgotten.

I went to the bathroom and flushed the napkin down the toilet. Then I went back into the living room.

"Well, Gus died," Dad said to Mom.

"Oh, no, really?" I said.

Dad looked surprised. "Leslie, you remember Gus?"

"Of course. He ate fire in Belmar," I said, and Mom nodded, laughing with me. "That was the best summer in my whole life." It was, too—though God knows it hadn't started out that way. It was right after Hilda left, and Dad was gone on a four-month tour, the longest he'd ever been away. They decided to send me to day camp—it would be "good" for me. I lasted three days and threw up six times, once on each trip. And I cried all the time in between. I don't know how long Mom would've made me keep going if the director hadn't made her take me out—I was expelled for being unhappy. Mom told me she cabled Dad in Hong Kong, saying, "Leslie refuses to go to camp. What shall I do?" and Dad cabled back, "Take her to Belmar." Dad had this sweet old aunt who ran a boardinghouse there, a block from the beach, and Mom rented a room for us

54

for the rest of that summer. It was wonderful. There was Uncle Gus and his wife, Sadie (they weren't really related to us)—Uncle Gus used to sit on the swing on the porch, set a ball of cotton on fire, and eat it. He could also find pennies behind my ears, and wiggle his scalp and ears at the same time. And Elsa, who sat in the sun from April till October every year and had skin the color of eggplant; she painted her fingernails silver, and they looked incredible, jumping out at you like phosphorescent seashells. And there were Frankie and Gilda and their three horrible kids, Gail, Dee Dee, and Grant. That was the regular crew, and others came and went, a week here, two weeks there.

Mom and I went to the beach every day. There was a snack bar, run by a beautiful silver-haired woman who had a sixteen-year-old daughter named Priscilla. But her nickname was Laura. Funny how you remember things like that; I mean, who cares? (I do, I guess.) They sold these ice-cream things called Rockets—vanilla fudge ice cream in a cylinder-shaped piece of cardboard with a stick at the bottom, which you pushed up. Mom and I called them Jets. And in the evenings Mom and I would walk to a lake nearby and watch the swans.

"Mom, did you know swans are a symbol of hypocrisy?" I said.

"What?"

"I was just thinking about the swans in Belmar, remember? Well, I was reading someplace about how swans used to be a symbol of hypocrisy in art because they have black flesh."

She shuddered. "Don't tell me that."

"I just did," I said with some satisfaction. "What did Gus die of?"

"Cancer," Dad said. "Well, he was seventy-eight."

"Yes, but it's always too soon," Mom said, sighing. Yes—it is, it's always too soon. Don't die—please don't die—if you die, I'll die. In fact, I'd *rather* die first, so I don't have to lose you.

I eyed the chocolates again and picked out one more to take with me to my room. Dad was reading the paper. Mom looked at me as though she were about to say something, then changed her mind.

"Finish your homework," she called.

I stuck my head around the side of the door, saying, "Mother, darling, I finished it ages ago. This is your wunderkind, remember?"

"My wunderkind who is flunking algebra!" she retorted cheerfully.

"So what? So did you. Anyway, I'm not *flunking*. Aren't I allowed an occasional C+?"

"Honeybunch, just passing that stuff is a miracle," she said, smiling at me.

"Hey! You love me?"

"To the moon and back."

I went into my room, trying to decide which record to do my evening sit-ups to. I finally decided on Jimmy Cliff and got down on my back. The first song was the best one to exercise to, and usually I just kept playing it over and over till I filled my quota. The song's called

"You Can Get It If You Really Want." Yes, I can, I thought, feeling like I had a private marching band in my head cheering me on. I know what I want. I want to be happy. And being happy means being thin. That's all I want. I don't ask for much. I never did. Mom always praised me because I hardly ever asked for anything the way other people's kids did, like clothes and stuff. And then, whenever I *did* ask for anything, of course I got it because "Leslie never asks for anything." But wanting things can be a tricky business. I don't know about other people, but once I set my heart on something, I just won't quit till I get it. Even if it starts looking like the wrong thing to go after, you know? I don't stop to question it; I just go for it, figuring once I've got it, I'll worry about the rest. Anyhow, I thought, I'm right about wanting to be thin. I've never been more certain of anything, ever. I got up to put the needle back to the beginning again and began doing jumping jacks for a breather.

"*Leslie*," Mom said, banging on the door. "The Serlings are going to call the police, and I won't blame them!" The Serlings lived in the apartment beneath ours.

"Yeah, yeah, OK," I said, switching to waist twists. If you weren't such a fat clod, said the dictator, you wouldn't thud like that. Only a few more pounds to go. How many pounds till I'm happy, how many pounds till I'm thin? Three more pounds till I'm skinny, three more pounds and I win! "Oh, ugh, Hiller," I whispered affectionately. "Cut the crap and twist."

Then one day at school the following week I went to the nurse.

"Hi, Miss Chase," I said. "Can I have some aspirin?"

"I think we can scrounge some up," she said, opening the small chest in the back of her office and handing me two aspirin in a little medicine cup. "I have Midol, if you prefer," she said.

I blinked at her, not knowing what she meant, and then said, "Oh, no, I just have a headache." Midol. What a laugh!

She nodded, then squinted at me, looking me up and down. "You've lost more weight." *Hey*, lady, no kidding? I thought. You're pretty sharp. "How much do you weigh now?"

"I don't know," I said truthfully. At that point it almost didn't matter; when I hit 105, I'll *know*, I thought, because I'll be thin. I won't need a scale to tell me.

"Well, we'll see," she said, taking my arm and hauling me over to the scale. I kicked off my loafers and got on, waiting to be judged.

She started out at 110, and I shut my eyes. Finally she stopped moving the metal weight, and I opened my eyes to look.

"One hundred and three," Miss Chase announced, putting her hands on her hips.

I stared at the numbers, pressing down as hard as I could. "Are you sure this scale is right?"

"Yes, Leslie, this scale is right," she said sternly. "And

103 pounds is entirely too little for someone of your height."

I got off the scale, feeling both elated and frightened. I don't understand, I thought. Miss Chase was still talking, but I wasn't listening. This doesn't make sense. I'm two pounds below my magic number, but things aren't perfect, and I'm still not thin. I must have made a mistake; 105 was the wrong number. Yeah, that's it. Maybe —99? Yikes! Under 100 pounds—beyond my wildest dreams! Surely I'll be thin at 99, I told myself; and maybe a couple of extra pounds off, so I'll have a margin for error.

"Leslie, you're not listening to me," Miss Chase said.

"I'm sorry. What did you say?"

"I *said*, you shouldn't lose any more weight. In fact, you could use a good five or ten pounds."

"Ha!" I said, laughing. "Are you kidding?"

"Now, Leslie . . ." she began, but I lifted my chin and turned, practically dancing out of her office.

"Thanks for the aspirin," I called, skipping down the long hall leading to the back stairs, which I took two at a time. That I should have lived to see the day someone would tell me to gain weight . . . Hiller, Hiller, I love you! Now, then, don't get carried away, came a warning voice. You still have a way to go. Yes, OK, well, since I weigh less, that means it takes fewer calories to maintain this weight, which means I have to start cutting down if I'm to keep losing. Breakfast will be two ounces of cottage cheese, not three. That's sixty calories. No lunch.

Dinner. They'll nag me. They nag me already. Come on, Hiller, *think*. I was so lost in thought, I knocked smack into Annie.

"Hey!" she said, too startled to whisper. She recovered, resumed her slouch, and gazed at me with her half-shut smoky green eyes. She's thinking what a fat clumsy jerk I am.

"Hey, are you high or something?" she said.

"You might say that," I said slyly. Why should I be intimidated by her just because she's got terrible posture, phony laryngitis, and is absolutely beautiful? I thought bravely. Stand up, Leslie. You're older, you're smarter; come on, kid.

"Yeah?" Annie said, looking impressed. "Hey, come on, no shit?"

Oh, Christ, Annie French, you really are too much. I cocked my head slightly, a faint smile beginning to tug at the corners of my cracked, vitamin-B-deficient lips.

"Yeah, Annie. I'm high from not eating."

"Hey, wow," she said. "You did lose a lot of weight. You really don't eat, huh?"

"It's the best way to lose weight. Wouldn't you say?" She looked at me, not knowing how to respond, and I laughed. I'm not scared of you, I thought. She pushed her hair out of her eyes, and it fell right back again.

"Cavett says you're a really good artist," she said. I shrugged modestly. "I'd like to see your work sometime."

"Annie," I said suspiciously, "why are you being so nice to me?"

She stared at me. "I've got a class," she said, and

began walking away. Then she turned around, giving me a friendly smile. "You're crazy, you know that?"

I went back to my study hall, and Cavett whispered, "What took you so long? I thought you fell in."

"I went to the nurse," I whispered back. "And then you'll never believe what happened."

"What?"

"Annie talked to me."

"Poor you."

"Cavett, she was actually nice. Nice for Annie, that is," I added. Then I remembered the scale. "Guess how much I weigh. 103!"

"Hey!" Cavett exclaimed, thumping me on the back. "Now you can *eat!*"

"Will you guys please *shush?*" Marla said, looking over her shoulder at us in annoyance.

"Sorry," Cavett said, making a horrible face as soon as her back was turned.

"No," I whispered to Cavett.

" 'No' what?"

"No, I can't eat. Not yet."

Cavett rolled her eyes. "Whaddya mean, not yet? *When* then?'

I was about to answer, and then I just shrugged and opened my book. When? When I'm thin, that's when. And I'll know when I'm thin because I'll be happy. Once in seventh grade when we were studying the Bible as Literature, I asked my teacher about the Messiah. "I bet there are lots of people who think they're the Messiah, like people who think they're Napoleon or something, but who believes them? I mean they all end up on the funny farm, right?" I said.

"I don't think I understand the question," Mrs. Atkins said.

"Well, I mean, what happens if the real Messiah comes along? What's the point in waiting for the Messiah if we'll just stick him in a psychiatric hospital?"

"When it's the genuine article, Leslie, everyone will know. That's what people believe."

"But *how* will they know?" I insisted.

She looked at me helplessly. "They just *will*."

Well, that's how it is with the weight, I thought. When I get to the right weight, I'll just *know* it. There isn't much point in having a goal anymore—I'll just keep going till I'm thin, that's all. I realized I'd been reading the same line in my book over and over again, and I had no idea what it said. We were reading *The Madwoman of Chaillot*. "To be alive is to be fortunate, Roderick," I read. Is it? I wondered. Is it really? Shame on you, Leslie! After what Mom went through to get you here?

"Cavett," I said, poking her. "Are your parents going to be home tonight?"

"They're going out to dinner with some people who're here from L.A. Why?"

"Can I come home with you? And stay till seven or so?" I said. "I don't want to be home for dinner."

"Sure, you can come, but how come you . . . Leslie, your fingernails!"

"*Shhh!*" Marla spat.

"Leslie, they're *blue!*" Cavett whispered, horrified.

62

"Yeah, I know. They get like that a lot. Hey, thanks about tonight," I said quickly. "You're a lifesaver." I grabbed my books, saying, "Gotta go to the library," and left.

Every night that week I managed to avoid dinner. An early baby-sitting job on Wednesday, a documentary I had to watch on Thursday evening for social studies, can I eat in my room? . . . Oh, Mom, I'm sorry, I had a hot dog in front of the Metropolitan Museum, and by the way, you really *must* see the Persian miniatures, they're exquisite. 100, 99, 98, 97, tick, tick, tick. This can't go on forever. One day I won't have an excuse, and what then? Throwing up is no good—I might not get it all out. Besides, I don't want the food in me even for a few minutes. I can't any more. What's a mother to do?

"Mom, Robin and I are going to Bloomingdale's tonight," I said the following Monday. "So I won't be home for dinner, OK?"

"Where will you eat?" she said.

"Blum's."

"Blum's went out of business," she said, putting her hands on my shoulders. Congrats, Leslie, you sure know how to pick 'em. "Leslie, did you have breakfast?"

"Of course!"

"Leslie, you've got to eat more. Look at you. Soon there'll be nothing left of you!" she said, her voice rising.

"I'm *fine*, Mom. Really I am."

"What did you eat for breakfast? Nothing!"

"I did too eat. I ate cottage cheese." Truth. "Mom, *please* don't worry about me! I'm fine!" Truth? "I feel great!" Lie. I pulled away from her. "I won't be late, OK?" She just looked at me, biting her lip. "I'll call you from Bloomingdale's to tell you when I'll be home."

She walked to the door with me. "What will you have for lunch? Wait—" She went back to the kitchen and came back with a brown paper bag. I peered into it. Yogurt. Poor Mom. She's playing on my terms now.

"Strawberry?" I said enthusiastically.

"Raspberry," she said, on the verge of tears. Should I laugh or cry? I thought, looking at her expression.

"Even better," I said, kissing her on the cheek. "Mom —Mom, I love you."

"I love you, too," she whispered.

I left and walked slowly to the bus stop. 7:45 A.M. I'm tired. Why am I so tired? Just before my bus came, I dropped the bag in the trash can. Sorry, Mom. God, I'm sorry.

CHAPTER SIX

I got off the bus at 59th and Lexington and spotted Robin across the street. I waited impatiently for the light to change, then trotted over to her.

"Robin." I tapped her shoulder. She turned around and looked at me as though I were a stranger. Then her mouth dropped open.

"Leslie?"

I nodded, feeling like an idiot.

"My God," she said, taking in her breath and looking me up and down. "I wouldn't have recognized you!"

"I'll take that as a compliment," I said dryly.

She didn't laugh. "Leslie, what *happened* to you? Have you been sick?"

"No," I said. My teeth began chattering. "Can we go inside? I'm cold."

"*Cold?* It's so nice out!" She saw my expression and mumbled, "Yeah, sure, let's go."

"I need jeans," I said when we got up to the third floor. "None of mine fit."

"I'm not surprised. What size do you take, negative-one?"

We hardly talked to each other for two hours. Robin started out telling me about her school, and what she'd been reading, and some bicycle trip she was going to take over the summer. I listened, but somehow I couldn't think of anything to say. I feel so far away, I thought; she's telling me these things as though they're important, and I don't understand. Did I use to care about things like that? I can't remember. No, that isn't true. I remember a girl with my name . . . but nothing matters anymore except this diet. Everything else kind of fades away now. After a while I noticed she'd stopped talking, but I was too exhausted to think about it. Getting around Bloomingdale's with all those mirrors and lights and loud music without breaking your neck is . . . I sound like my mother, I thought. "Nothing worse should ever happen!" she'd say. Robin kept giving me odd looks.

"What's wrong?" I said once, catching her staring at me as I went through one of the sale racks.

"Nothing," she said, looking bewildered.

Finally I found a pair of jeans in the boys' department.

"Thank God," I groaned. Suddenly everything began swaying, including me.

She grabbed my arm, looking frightened. "Are you OK?"

I leaned back against the wall and slid down to a crouch. "This store," I said, shaking my head and trying to laugh. "I'm seasick. My mother won't even come in

66

anymore. She goes into a panic. Bloomingdale's is a health hazard, it really is."

We hardly spoke on the bus home. Then, right before we came to my stop, Robin took a deep breath and said, "Leslie, you're not the same person."

I sat up. "I *am!*" I looked at her face, and my eyes filled with tears.

"Oh, Leslie," she said softly. "What's wrong? Please tell me!"

"I don't know. I don't know!"

And then my stop came. I went to the door, looked back at her once, and suddenly found myself racing through the dark streets like a hunted animal. "You-can-get-it-if-you-really-want-but-you-must-try-try-and-try." What's wrong? Nothing's wrong, nothing's wrong, and asking is against the rules. You want to know what's wrong? Seeing Robin, that's what's wrong, but otherwise everything's fine. I'm fine, Mom. I love you, I do, I do, so what's wrong? What's the matter?

"Everything all right, miss?"

I stopped dead in my tracks. A policeman was looking at me curiously. "Someone after you?"

"No." Yes. No.

"Just getting into shape, huh?"

"Right," I said. Right, that's it. I'm getting into shape. Run, Hiller. Run. Burn up those calories. You're fat. This excess flesh has to go. He said I'm getting into shape. That must mean I look like I need to. Run! This little piggy ran all the way home! I love you, Mom.

I'm sorry for every time I ever got mad at you. Because I love you and someday you'll be dead. Can you forgive me? No, I don't know what for, but I apologize anyway. Why did I go shopping with Robin? Who needs to be treated like a freak? Who needs her, who needs anyone? Who needs friends when you've got a mother like mine?

Two tablespoons equal one ounce. One ounce of cottage cheese for breakfast then. I don't really need two whole ounces. One pack of Trident for lunch, 3.8 calories per piece. Dinner. . . . What's dinner?

96, 95, 94, who's counting? (Me, that's who.) Maybe all of this will improve my math—my head is filled with numbers all day long.

One night the inevitable happened: I couldn't wangle my way out of sitting at the dinner table. Dad was leaving for Scotland the next day for a 3½-week tour.

"I want to have dinner with my family on my last night at home," he said adamantly.

Gee, Dad, I don't see what the big deal is—you're always leaving. I'm used to that. Aren't you? It's OK with me, really it is. At least I know you're happy. And I'm not always afraid you'll get hurt. Weird how I worry more about something happening to Mom, who never goes anywhere. Damn it, how am I going to handle dinner? If I keep dropping food into my lap and down to Harry, he'll end up with a heart condition. That's all I need, more guilt. Curiosity didn't kill the cat, Leslie did. Besides, Sammy catches me doing it one out of four times, and he has a habit of reporting everything. On-the-spot and up-to-the-minute. What a pain he is.

"Mommy tells me you don't want to go to your art class any more," Dad said to me. I wish you wouldn't chew with your mouth open, I thought, watching him in silent annoyance.

"Nah," I said finally, shoving a meatball around my plate. "I don't really like the emphasis they put on having things in proportion. It's all so mechanical."

"But isn't that important?" he said. "An artist needs to know these things before they can go on to do other things."

"You're right . . . I don't know, maybe I should just switch to a different class . . ." I trailed off. It was true I was tired of hearing that the torso should be three times the size of the head—or was it four?—but the main reason I wanted to quit was I was too tired to go to my class. It was too much of an effort. Nearly everything is, these days, I thought idly.

"Leslie, eat your meat," Dad said. So it's starting, I thought nervously.

"Is it good?" Mom asked him.

"Delicious."

"You always say that," she complained.

"And is that so terrible?" he said, laughing. He glanced at me. "Leslie, you're not eating."

I put a huge piece of meat in my mouth, shoving it over to one side. "This needs salt," I said, jumping up and running into the kitchen. I spit the meat into my hand and threw it away, returning with the salt shaker.

"I never put in enough salt," Mom apologized.

Sammy began chattering about some teacher he hated, and I tuned out, shoving my food around some more.

"Leslie, you're not eating," Mom said.

"I'm full," I said, tensing up.

"Full? How can you be full? How can a person who doesn't eat be full?"

"Full of what, air?" Dad followed up. "You're going to make yourself sick, Leslie."

"No, I'm not. I eat when I'm hungry," I said, clenching my fists in my lap. "I'm not going to eat when I'm not hungry. That's how people get fat."

"Fat? She's worried about being fat?" Mom looked at me and then at Dad. You're goddamn right I am, and high time, too. If you had your way, I'd still be a fat slob.

"What's this 'she' crap?" I snapped. "I'm *here*, aren't I?" I turned to Dad. "Tell her to stop, will you? She gets all worked up over nothing."

"Max," Mom pleaded.

I watched her, waiting. She's going to cry. Wait . . . wait . . . there she goes. Like a faucet. "Why do you cry over everything?" I shouted. "You cry all the time! This is ridiculous!" She began to shake. "It's not *my* fault you were hungry when you were a kid! My eating won't change that!"

"Leslie," she begged. "Of course it's not your fault. You're my child, and I'm worried about you. I can't help that!"

"If you don't want to eat for yourself, then eat one meatball to please your mother," Dad said.

"No."

"You won't eat one lousy meatball to please your mother?" he yelled, picking up my fork and spearing a piece of meat. I got up from my chair and began backing away. They've gone mad, I thought. They've all gone mad. I looked over at Sammy; his eyes were like two saucers, mouth open, mashed potatoes all over his tongue.

"Daddy, stop it," I said quietly.

"To please *me* then!" he said.

"No. No, no, no, no, no!" I began to cry. "No," I whimpered, turning and walking down the hall to my room. God, if you're there, don't let them follow me, I thought. Also don't let me pass out. "No," I whispered, my body beginning to shake with sobs. Mom came up behind me. "Leave me alone," I cried. "Just leave me alone!" Crying is against the rules, Hiller. You're strong, don't let them break you. They're trying to destroy you. Well, it won't work. You won't let it happen.

"If you're upset about something, then let's talk about it, Leslie," Mom said, trying to control herself. "We're not trying to make you unhappy."

"You may not be *trying* to but you *are*," I said, brushing away my tears in embarrassment. Leslie never cries, remember? Leslie never asks for things, and Leslie never cries.

"Then I'm sorry. I'm trying to understand . . ." Mom said, wringing her hands.

"I know, Mom."

"We only want you to be happy and healthy. We love you so very much."

"You want me to be happy?" I challenged.

"Yes," she said, startled. "Of course I do. We do."

"Well, I can't be happy unless I'm thin." Strike. I sat down on my bed. I'm glad Dad's leaving; it'll be a lot easier with him away. No more tears, Leslie; everything will be OK.

"Leslie," Mom said, trying to sound calm, "when is this dieting going to stop?"

That's easy, I thought. "See this?" I said, grabbing the flesh beneath my rib cage. "See it? When that's gone —that's when I'll stop."

She stood there silently for a moment, then turned and left, closing my door behind her.

Late that night I tiptoed into the living room to look for Mom's collection of Emily Dickinson poems, and I saw a small strip of light across the dining-room floor. Did they forget to turn the kitchen light off? I wondered. Or are they in there? I crept over to the door and heard Dad mumbling something. Then I heard him say, "What's her name?"

"Diane Jenkins."

"Doctor?"

"No, she's a psychologist," Mom said. My mouth fell open in amazement. They said a few things I couldn't hear, and I held my breath.

"Max, she made me feel like I was crazy. Do you know what she said? She said, 'I'm not worried about

72

your daughter, Mrs. Hiller. I'm worried about *you*.' "

"Are you . . ." Dad began.

"I'm going to see her again next week. Oh, Max, *am* I crazy? I don't know, tell me! There's just something not right . . ." Then she mumbled something else I couldn't hear. ". . . wish you weren't going now, I can't cope."

Dad sighed. "I'm sorry, Ruth. You know I am. I'm sure she'll be fine. Look, maybe we're overreacting. I'm sure many teenaged girls go on diets . . ." There was a long silence. Then I heard them get up, and I scampered back to my room and shut the door silently.

So she went to a shrink, I thought. Wow. And the shrink told her she's the one that needs help. So nothing's the matter with me? How strange it is, other people don't have to do what I'm doing, yet they manage to like themselves enough to keep going. Why can't I be like them? But I'm not. I don't do this because I want to— I have to. Follow the rules, Hiller, I'm only looking out for you. Mom says she wants me to be happy. I want that, too, but I can't be happy if I eat . . . you ought to understand, Mom. You're not happy when you buy nice clothes or when people give you gifts. You won't even take your lousy iron-supplement pills. Isn't that a kind of starving? And don't you get something out of it? Something—more? Being stingy is fun, Mom. It's like a game.

I went to bed without even attempting any sit-ups. I can't, I'd told the dictator several days before. I just can't anymore. And it was OK. I got a break. Sometimes the dictator lets things go; the important thing, after all, was not to eat, and I was OK in that department. Aren't I allowed an occasional C+?

The next morning I awoke to find a letter on my rug, which Mom had shoved under the door. I picked it up and sat on the radiator, looking out at the park. Brown. Burnt umber, with patches of white snow, like a cow, and little colored dots moving slowly around the football field. Joggers. Finally I unfolded the letter.

Leslie,

Never wonder about my love for you. I know I'm a terrible nag sometimes, but it is only because I love you so very much and want so much to *make* you happy, not only to see you happy. We are so lucky to have such a rare, wonderful human being for a daughter. You are talented and intelligent and beautiful. I can hardly wait to see all your accomplishments as you grow up—and even if you decide to do nothing but drink Tab all day, you'll still be the first star in our firmament because there is no better friend to me in the whole entire world. You feel for people, and with people, and me especially, more acutely and understandingly than people four times your age. If I am difficult these days, it is only because I am worried about you. Your happiness means everything to me. Please forgive this crazy Jewish mother!

XXX Mom

I read the letter over again I don't know how many times before I left for school. It's hard to explain—it was like hearing a chord with one wrong note. This is such a beautiful letter, I thought. She loves me. She thinks I'm fantastic and talented . . . she says she'll love me even if I turn out to be a flop . . . because . . . why was it, again? Oh . . . because I feel *for* people, and *with* people, and her especially . . . isn't that a good thing? Isn't it? My happiness means everything to her . . . but I haven't any happiness left, Mommy. And now, to make it worse, I can't even be grateful! What kind of awful person am I to try to find fault with a letter anyone, anyone would want to receive? Why do I keep hearing what Dad calls a clinker?

For one fleeting instant I thought of showing the letter to Cavett, then dismissed the idea. How could I show her something like this? I thought. Mom would die! But how would she know? She wouldn't have to. I'd know, and that's enough. Good God, Hiller, your head is like a little courtroom. I'm the accused, the defendant, the attorney for the defense, the prosecuting attorney—and the judge is a great big scale.

"Sorry I'm late, Miss Cole," I mumbled, walking slowly into biology class.

"That's all right, Leslie."

We had biology three times a week. Three times a week I was late. The lab was on the top floor of the school building, and the class that met before biology was on the first floor. And walking up took longer every day. Miss Cole never complained. I don't know what she thought, but I guess it was obvious I wasn't having the time of my life.

"Celia, can I borrow your blazer again?" I whispered. "I'm freezing."

"Sure," she said, taking it off the back of her chair and handing it to me. I kind of liked Celia. Her parents were divorced, and she lived on Sutton Place with her fabulously wealthy father and his 26-year-old wife, whom Celia claimed to be crazy about. I think she was probably lonely, even lonelier than I was—I had Cavett, and she didn't really have anyone. I put on her blazer and slumped down in my chair, taking my pack of Trident out of my knapsack and opening it.

"Hey, can I have a piece?" she whispered.

I looked over at her. Leslie, it's five pieces or none, the dictator said. All or nothing. When you make a decision, you stick to it. If you had three pieces, or four, it would be because of Celia, and no longer because of *you*. And you can't say no to her—the thought made me sick. How do you explain to someone that giving them your lousy sugarless gum means giving them half your daily allotment of food? You, Celia, probably had eggs for breakfast, a sandwich for lunch, and will have who knows what for dinner. I wish I could tell you—

"Here, take the whole pack," I said.

"Oh, no, Leslie, I just wanted one piece," she said. "Really."

"No, take it," I said, handing it to her. "I don't really like cinnamon much anyway." She looked at me doubtfully. "Here! Jeez, it's only gum."

"Well, OK," she said. "Thanks."

Yeah, sure. You bet. Leslie, you didn't really need that Trident anyway. Discontinued from this moment forth. And no one must ever know how greedy you really are. My stomach twisted as though someone were wringing it for a last drop. Empty. It hurts. Feel it eating itself? Chewing at itself, burning itself, twisting around in a silent agonizing dance? Now I know what a starved wolf must feel like. Prowling around, ready to kill, tearing away at raw flesh. This is not like other hunger, as in "I'm so hungry. I haven't eaten all day." I'm not hungry anymore, I thought; I'm way beyond hunger. I feel like a savage. And it scares the hell out of me.

Yes, and I know what a rat feels like. Bread crusts in the garbage tempt me. There's nothing I wouldn't scavenge. But even garbage is too good for me. I thought of a movie I once saw, a German propaganda film from World War II. In it there were alternating strips of film. One shot would show Jews eating, the next would show rats, and it switched back and forth—to show the resemblance between Jews and rats. It made me sick to see it. I'd thrown up afterward. But those people were *good* people, I told myself. Those people were *my* people. Good, kind people, the people Mom cries about. *I'm* the rat. *I'm* the one who ought to be dead, not them!

"Hey, Leslie," Celia whispered. "You look like you're going to cry."

Feeling dazed, I turned toward her and shook my

77

head no. Everything in this room is so bright, I thought, looking around. It almost hurts to look at it. Things sound different, too—as though everyone were talking into a tin can. Not just louder, you know? Tinny.

After class, Miss Cole caught me by the arm as I was leaving. "Leslie, you don't look well. You don't look well at all."

I shrugged, not knowing what to say, but I was moved. Miss Cole was a real cut-and-dried spinster, and not a particularly inspiring teacher, though I'll grant you, it would have taken a court jester to get me interested in biology. And she was the last person you'd expect would take a personal interest in her students.

"You've lost a great deal of weight," she said. "How much do you weigh now?"

I shrugged again, and she squinted at me as though I were a specimen under her microscope.

"Why don't you go see Miss Chase?" she said. Oh, please, give me a break. The last thing I want is the school nurse bugging me. "If you won't, I will," she said. "I'm worried about you, Leslie. Does your mother—" Does my mother what? I thought, waiting for her to finish. She didn't seem to know, either.

"I'm fine, Miss Cole," I said, pulling away from her. "I really am. It's nice of you to worry about me, but I'm fine. Honest." I opened the door and left.

With Dad gone, I knew the time had come to fix the dinner situation. I couldn't face having to come up with a new excuse every night, terrified I wouldn't be able to

and have Mom get hysterical. I can't fake it anymore—
she's onto me. And she's scared. Scared enough for me
to get away with this.

"Mom," I said that Friday night. "Mom, listen. I can't
eat in front of you."

"Why?"

"I don't know why, I just can't," I said. Then I began
to cry. "Please, Mom, let me eat dinner in my room—
please!" Leslie who never cries is crying.

"Well . . ." she said desperately.

"Please, Mom! Please, I promise to eat if you let me
eat in my room—"

What else could she do? She knew I wouldn't eat at
the table, but there was a chance I'd eat alone.

"You promise?" she said.

"Have I ever given you any reason to mistrust me?"
It's so easy to lie when you're trusted implicitly—and it
feels so degrading. I'm desperate—I never thought I
could feel this desperate.

"No, you haven't," she conceded. "OK."

Lamb chops. What in God's name am I going to do
with them? I can't flush them down the toilet—she'll
hear; she'll know. I can't put them in the garbage. They'll
smell, and Harry will drag them out and give me away.
There must be a way to get rid of them! I cut the meat off
the bone and shoved it around the plate to make it look
as though I'd eaten. The aroma was too much for me.
You, I thought, staring at it—I hate you. You're dis-
gusting. You're trying to seduce me. You're trying to kill
me! The desk lamp shone on the plate, like a lamp in

an operating room. Hey, Leslie, I thought, turning away from the food. Hey, kid, you sound bonkers. How can you hate a lamb chop? I gazed out the window; the moon was full. Mom used to think the moon was God. She used to sing me a song that said, "I see the moon, the moon sees me." Hey, peppermint-in-the-sky, are you watching me? I'm freezing, I thought. No wonder; Mom opened my other window again. As I went over to close it, it hit me. The other window faces Central Park West, but *this* one faces the courtyard . . . nobody ever goes out there. Nobody will ever know.

I took a Kleenex and put all but two small pieces of meat and half the asparagus into it, went to the window, and tossed it. I plugged my fingers in my ears for about ten seconds, then picked up my plate and opened the door.

Mom met me halfway to the kitchen. "How was it?" she said haltingly.

"It was great, Mom." Truth. I'm telling her the truth. I'm *sure* those lamb chops were great.

CHAPTER ·SEVEN

Someone was screaming at me in German, and I couldn't understand a word she was saying. I ran out, terrified, and fell down a flight of stairs, landing in a dark room. Huddled in the corner was an Orthodox Jewish man, praying. But he was praying on his knees. I began walking toward him hesitantly, and suddenly he became a woman. She looked at me, eyes filled with hate, and she opened her mouth and began to throw up. I tried to scream and woke up, fists clenched so hard they hurt. I turned on my night table lamp and looked at the clock: 2:00 A.M..

I got out of bed and sat on the radiator, trying to warm up. It hurts to sit without cushions. Whoever heard of a bony ass? And of course, there was no heat. Wrapping a small plaid blanket around my shoulders, I walked over to the mirror, moving like an old, arthritic woman. God, I feel so sick. Why? Nauseated and cold, so cold, and so tired. Am I thin yet? The mirror certainly doesn't tell me anything nowadays . . . I'm so cold I never even look at myself undressed. I get dressed and undressed in bed, under the covers. I have no idea what I look like. It doesn't seem to matter anymore. My eyes look bigger, I thought, staring at my face; my lips are cracked in both corners and won't heal. My hair isn't wavy any more; it sort of wilts . . . what's left of it. My collarbone sticks out farther, I guess—I don't know what I look like, I don't even know what I *want* to look like anymore. All the thin people I used to wish I looked like weigh at least twenty-five pounds more than I do— and still they're thinner. I don't understand. Is there something wrong with me? What, though? Would anyone believe what I'm doing? I didn't plan it this way . . . I had no idea.

I went to my desk, opened the drawer, and took out a pair of scissors, paper, and a tin of colored pencils. I cut the paper into a heart shape and picked up a pen, thinking. Finally I wrote:

Dear Mom,

I love you. You're the best mother anyone could hope to have. Don't worry about me. Trust me—I *am* to be trusted. I can't help it if I want to be skinny so much that I'll do anything to succeed. Please don't worry so much!

Love, Leslie

There. I began to draw little colored hearts all over it. Blue, yellow, orange, lavender, red, turquoise, pink, magenta . . . every time I thought I was finished, there was another white space commanding me to fill it. What time is it? I wondered, not looking at the clock. I remember . . . asking Hilda that. In the evenings, waiting for Mom to come home. Every five minutes from six on, until at last she came. Or did she? Then why do I feel as though I'm still waiting, waiting for Mom to come home? My hand began to ache, and I realized I was pressing so hard I'd broken the red pencil tip. The clock said 3:40. I picked up the note, afraid of looking at it, and placed it on the rug beside my bed. So I won't forget. I turned off the light and pulled the blanket over my head, curling into a tight ball and breathing into my cupped hands. Where should I leave this note so I'm certain, absolutely certain she'll find it? On the hall table, or in her purse, or—in the refrigerator. Of course. That's where I'll put it.

Then I did something I hadn't done since I was five years old. I checked my pillowcase to see whether the open-ended side was facing the wall. Every night for a year after Mom quit work, as soon as I got into bed, I'd check to see if the open-ended side of my pillowcase was facing the wall. And if it was, I turned it the other way. It was kind of like magic—I'd pretend that home was in between the wall and the pillow, and if the closed side was next to the wall, it meant Mom couldn't get out. People could come *in*, but they couldn't leave.

I uncurled and reached for the wall side of my pillow with my left hand. It was closed side in. . . . Where will I leave the heart note so she'll see it as *soon* as she opens the fridge, first thing? I know: the egg compartment. I lifted my pillow and, in one quick motion, flopped it over, open side facing the wall. Then I fell asleep.

"Leslie, I had a phone call from Barrow today," Mom said one evening. "Miss Krebbs."

"Uh-oh, what did I do?"

"Nothing. Apparently several of your teachers have told her that they're—concerned about you."

"But I'm doing fine," I said defensively. "Even in math. I'm doing my work—"

"I told her that," Mom broke in. "She said they're not worried about your grades, they're worried about *you*."

"They're crazy, then."

"Hey, *Ma*," Sammy called from his room. A moment later he appeared. "You said you'd come in . . . " he began, then stopped short. "But it's OK, you can come later." Sammy never acts like that. Sammy, who'll fight me tooth and nail for Mom's attention. Only lately he doesn't fight with me. He almost seems scared of me—when I notice him.

"I'm sorry, Sammy," I called after him. "We'll be done talking in a sec, OK?"

"Take your time, no problem," he called back, and then there was silence. Finally we heard his door shut, and Mom glanced at me nervously, looking down at her hands as she spoke.

"Leslie, darling, you remember I once told you about a woman, a Dr. Jenkins, who gave a speech at a parent-teacher meeting several years ago?" I nodded. "Yes, well, I've been to see her several times because I felt I needed . . . someone to talk to, and I wondered whether perhaps . . . would you like to see her yourself?"

"Yes," I said without thinking. "Yes. I'll see her."

"Good," Mom said, looking surprised. Her face relaxed for a moment, then became taut again. "Leslie, I've also made an appointment for you to have a check-up."

"*Oh*, no. I'm *not* going to Dr. Polaski—"

"No, no, don't worry," she interrupted hurriedly. "You're seeing my doctor, Dr. Lese." She stopped, waiting for me to give her an argument. I was silent. "And then if you don't like him for some reason, or maybe you just won't want to have the same doctor as I have, he can recommend somebody else. OK?"

"Yeah," I said. "Fine, Mom." I don't understand myself, Mom. You're so considerate you even worry I may want a different doctor from you, and yet . . . I don't know, there's something wrong . . . but it must be in me.

You expected me to fight, I guess. I'd never have fought. I'd never have *asked*, but I'd never have fought. I know—it surprises me, too. Don't get me wrong—I won't change. But if they can give me a pill to make things go back to the way they used to be—I'll take it.

Double-decker-doctor day, I thought as I stared at the clock that Thursday morning. It was ten-thirty. No school today. Mom tapped at my door and opened it a crack.

"Time to get up," she said.

"OK."

"Can I make you some eggs?" she offered timidly. I groaned inwardly. Mom! When are you going to get this straight? Haven't you caught on? "I bought a Teflon pan," she continued. "I can make them without butter . . ."

I shook my head no and closed my eyes until I heard the door shut. The innocent. Innocent, what a nice word. Hopeful. Not naïve . . . naïve implies lack of experience. Innocent is something else again; it's hoping, believing in things in spite of experience. Oh, Mom—how I want your eggs, and how I hate them! And how I hate my wants—what wants? the dictator whispered. You have no wants. You have no needs. You need nothing outside yourself. Nothing.

Dr. Jenkins came into the waiting room, and I stood up and shook hands with her.

"May I have a few minutes with you after . . ." Mom said to her, looking almost triumphant as Dr. Jenkins discreetly cased me up and down. You see? I could almost hear Mom saying. What did I tell you?

"Yes, of course," she said graciously, and I followed her into her office.

"Well, Leslie," she began, "why don't you tell me a bit about yourself?"

"Well—I guess my mother told you about my dieting," I said. That's what she means I should tell her about. That's how I got here. "I went on this diet in December, after I had the flu . . . " It didn't take long to tell her. She scribbled away the whole time I talked.

"And what about now?" she said when I came to a stop.

"You mean what do I eat now?" She nodded. "First, I have to ask you something. You wouldn't tell my mother anything I tell you, would you?"

"No, Leslie. Whatever you tell me is confidential."

"Really?" I said. "You promise? No matter what I tell you, you wouldn't repeat it?"

"I give you my word."

I decided to risk trusting her. "Well, uh—breakfast is usually three curds of cottage cheese—"

"Three what?"

"Curds, you know—" I did a little drawing in the air with my finger. "Uh, no lunch or anything—and then, my mother lets me have dinner in my room. . . ." Oh, Christ, am I doing the right thing? I thought. But I can't lie. Maybe if I tell her, then things will get fixed. She can't fix things if I lie.

"Yes? What about dinner?" she prompted.

"I don't eat dinner," I said, looking at my sneakers. "I lie to her. I tell her I've eaten it, but I never do."

"What do you do with it?"

"I throw it out the window."

"You throw it out the window," she repeated. I nodded. "How much do you weigh now, Leslie?"

"I don't know. I'm going to my mom's doctor later. . . ." She's weirded-out, I thought. She doesn't know what to make of me any more than I do.

"And when do you plan to begin eating again?" she said curiously.

"I—don't." It sounded so strange; it was the first time I'd said it out loud. "I used to think I'd eat again when I got thin, but now . . . I can't imagine eating."

"But if you don't eat, they'll have to put you in the hospital and tube-feed you."

I held my hands out, palms up. "OK," I said. "If that's what they have to do. I'm not going to eat."

"Do you think this may be a way of trying to kill yourself?"

"No," I said thoughtfully. "No, I don't *think* that's what I'm trying to do. Sometimes I think I don't deserve to live . . . but mainly it's that I *can't* live unless I do this."

She stared at me, not saying anything.

Mom saw her for about fifteen minutes, while I sat in the empty waiting room, staring at the wall. Then Mom came out, took my hand lightly in hers, and we left.

"Hello there," Dr. Lese said jovially as he entered the examining room. I was sitting on the table in my underwear, freezing to death. Purple all over. He poked; he thumped; he listened to my heart, took my blood pressure twice, listening intently. The nurse stood by in silence, watching.

"When did you begin menstruating?" he said.

"When I was thirteen, but I stopped getting my period in November. My mother may have told you—"

"Mm, yes, she mentioned that." He glanced quickly

at my chart. "You saw Dr. Chester," he said, smiling. "He and I went to Yale together. We belong to the same tennis club."

"Oh?" I said politely.

"And he recommended—uh huh, mm," he mumbled, reading the rest of whatever was there. "OK, let's see what you weigh."

Down off the table, over to the scale. I wasn't afraid; just tired. I can only weigh less, so it's OK. Up you go, kid.

"Wait a minute," I said, looking at the numbers. *"Thirty-nine?"*

"This scale is in kilos," he said distractedly, looking at me as though seeing me for the first time. "To get the weight in pounds you multiply by 2.2. So 39 kilos equals about . . . 86 pounds."

"85.8," I corrected him.

"Let's get your height," he said. Last ditch effort, buster? It won't work. I'm not four feet ten. You'll see.

"Five feet five and a half inches tall," he reported. He stared at me again, then cleared his throat and said, "You can get dressed now, and I'll speak to you in my office."

"Fine," I said obediently.

Mom sat next to me in the taxi home looking like a shock victim. I can't believe this is going on, I thought. The whole thing is so outrageous. "Go home, try to gain a few pounds, and I'll see you again in two weeks," he'd told me before I left.

"But what if she loses *more* weight?" Mom had said.

"We'll cross that bridge when and if we come to it, Mrs. Hiller."

Granted, I lied. I didn't tell him I was providing the alley cats and rats with Delmonico steaks. But how sharp do you have to be to figure out I can't be telling the truth? I told Jenkins the truth, and I'd die if she betrayed my trust—but won't I die if she doesn't? What kinds of lunatics am I surrounded by? I feel like a mute, helpless. Nobody hears me; nobody sees me; nobody's listening to me. They poke and call and worry and ask me questions, but nobody can see or hear me; maybe I don't exist then. When I used to throw up, it made me feel free, at least for a while—free of tension, and fear, and free of *her*. But maybe all I've done is made more room for her inside me. I don't know—I don't know which I want! I want both!

"Eighty-six pounds," Mom whispered. "Eighty-six pounds. Leslie, I weighed 105 after the war when I had tuberculosis!"

"That's very thin," I said.

When she saw I wasn't being sarcastic, she clammed up. Yes, Mom, I know there's something off kilter, but I don't know what to do or say or ask for. Just keep going, Leslie—you've got a free two weeks. You'll coast.

Oh, God, can't somebody help me?

After that, time seemed to lose all meaning. Ten minutes felt like a week, and then a day would pass without my having noticed. I felt as though I were living in a

90

spiral vacuum, waiting to be sucked away, and until then, life was stark, a matter of survival. How can I think about looks or boys, rain or Easter vacation, how can I care about nuance or the color of the leaves I used to paint, when the questions I face are as black and white as "Will I make it to the bus stop, or will I fall down dead before I get there?"

The girls at school treated me gingerly, as though I were a time bomb and might go off any second. So silly, I thought; there's nothing for them to be afraid of. I'm totally undangerous. If I get mugged, that'll be it. I can't even run away. I'm quite harmless now, you see. To you. And now nobody can hurt me on the inside. I have this trick—anything you can do to me, I do to myself already. And I hit harder than you ever could.

Only Cavett continued to treat me as she always had. She had the most astonishing vision I've ever seen in anyone. Before this diet began, she used to offer me a brownie five minutes after I'd told her I wanted to lose weight; and if I said no, that was fine, and if I said yes, that was fine, too. Now, if she was eating an apple or a sandwich, she'd offer me a bite—and I said no, and she accepted it. It just didn't seem to matter much what I ate or didn't eat or what I looked like.

"Leslie," she said to me on Friday, six days before my next appointment with Dr. Lese. "Listen, I have to go to the Met this afternoon for European history. Do you want to go with me?" she said hopefully.

"Cavett, I can't," I said. "I wish I could . . . I'm so sorry."

"Hey, it's OK," she said. "The museum isn't shutting down, we'll go another time. How come you can't go?"

"I'd never make it up those stairs. It's all I can do to get home."

"Oh, I wish I could help you!" she burst out suddenly, her eyes clouding.

"Cavett, I didn't even think you noticed stuff like that," I said, touching her arm.

"Of course I notice! But what can I do? I'm not going to nag you like your mother does, that won't help, and besides you'd hate me if I did."

"Cavett, you know something? Usually I don't care that I'm too weak to do anything—there's nothing I want to do. But you make me mind not being able to. You make me think I'm missing something."

"Yeah, well, I don't know about you, but I sure am. There's nobody to do anything with—things aren't as much fun now that we never go places or anything," she said, looking down at her feet.

"You like me, don't you?"

"*Yeah*, I like you." She blushed. "I'm not too good at telling people I care about how I feel. I guess I get embarrassed or something," she mumbled. "But I mean you're my best friend, you know? I want you to be stronger, so we can do stuff again."

"What did you do last year, before I came?"

"Not very much. I was lonely."

I wanted to tell her I loved her, right then, but I knew how embarrassed she'd be, so I kept quiet.

"Have you thought of maybe seeing a shrink or something?" she said.

"I did, last week." I looked at her helplessly. "She didn't really say anything . . . I don't know. I just don't know."

Monday morning I woke up, and I knew I couldn't make it. I got out of bed, blacked out as usual, waited till I could see straight, then went to the bathroom, barely lifting my feet off the floor as I walked. It's hardly worth the trip, I thought; hardly anything comes out of me anymore. I looked at my face in the mirror; my skin looked absolutely green.

I walked to Mom's bedroom, opened the door, and stood there. She turned over in bed, and seeing me, she gave a start.

"What's the matter?"

"Mom, I can't go to school today."

"Why not?"

I stared at her dully. Tell her the truth, Leslie. She knows it anyway, and it doesn't even matter. "Because I don't think I can make it to the bus stop."

I stayed in bed until Thursday, barely conscious, waking up only to go to the bathroom and to throw away the dinners Mom brought on a tray. You'll never stop hoping, will you, Mom? I guess that's why you're here. Isn't it strange—how you keep cooking dinners for me and half believe I'm eating them, how I keep throwing them out and half believe I'll live forever. Will you cable Daddy in Scotland in a burst of clear vision, even though there's no one to tell you I'm miserable, saying, "Leslie refuses to eat. What shall I do?" Where can you take me this time? But you won't have to cable Daddy. He's coming home Thursday night—the night of my appointment with Dr. Lese. I wonder how much weight I've gained.

CHAPTER EIGHT

Seventy-six pounds," Dr. Lese said as I stood on the scale, multiplying in my head: $34.6 \times 2.2 = 76.12$. I'm not 76 yet, not quite yet, I thought. My secret. "Leslie, sit down," he said, motioning toward the examining table. I wobbled over and climbed up, too dazed to care that I was practically naked. "Do you know what you look like?" I shrugged, and he lifted my wrist. My hand flopped down, dangling limp as a fish. "Look at the size of your wrist." I looked, seeing nothing unusual. It is, after all, only a wrist, I thought; I never paid much attention to it before. Does it look different? He searched my face, trying to elicit some response, and finally said, "All right, Leslie, get dressed and come into my office."

When I went in, Mom was sitting in a chair, waiting for me. I sat in the chair next to hers, and we looked across the huge desk, waiting for God to speak.

"Leslie has lost ten more pounds," he said to Mom.

She blanched. "Her blood pressure is sixty-nine over fifty—"

"What does that mean?" Mom said, her voice quavering.

"It's extremely low, Mrs. Hiller. In view of the last two weeks . . . I think that we're going to have to hospitalize her."

Mom nodded, twisting her hands in her lap. She looked at me cautiously. "Leslie . . . ?"

"OK," I said. "Fine."

Dr. Lese's face relaxed somewhat. "I'm glad you're being so cooperative, Leslie." Hey, are you kidding? I'm so tired I don't care if I never get out of bed again.

"What section of the hospital will I be in?" I said.

"We have a ward for people on special diets, where everything you take in and put out is measured and weighed very carefully. I'll call and see if there's a bed available for tomorrow."

"What will you write in as my diagnosis?"

"We're not certain of that yet, Leslie. I know a very smart woman I'm going to speak to about you, and I think—" He turned to Mom. "It would be a good idea if Leslie sees her. She's very highly thought of. You mentioned Leslie had seen someone else, a Dr. Jenkins?"

"I'd rather see this one," I said to Mom. "If she's smart—"

"Yes, yes," Mom agreed hurriedly. "What's her name?"

"Dr. Elaine Sussman."

Mom and I looked at each other; then Mom stood up.

"Shall I call you later in the day about when to admit her?" she said.

"Yes, if you call at around . . . four-thirty, I'll have the information by then."

I opened my eyes, squinting. Someone had turned on the light.

"Daddy."

He came over and took my face in his hands, kissing my forehead.

"Did Mommy tell you?"

"Yes." He sat down on the edge of my bed. "Leslie. What have you done to yourself?"

"I don't know."

"Can't you help what you're doing?" I looked at him anxiously. Please don't get upset, Dad. I can't bear it. I can't cope. "No, I suppose if you could help it, we wouldn't be in the shape we're in now," he said, more to himself than to me.

"We?" I said, puzzled.

"Of course," he said. "Of course, 'we.' If you're sick or unhappy, it's our problem, too. We're a family, Leslie. You're our daughter."

"Oh." Why do my hands hurt? I thought, becoming aware that my fists were clenched. My whole body felt like a drum.

"Don't worry," he said, trying to read my expression. "It will all work out. I'm an optimist. The glass is always half full."

I managed a feeble smile, and he patted the blanket lightly, touching my thigh. A look of pain came across his face; then he said, "You go back to sleep now. I'll see you in the morning."

"How will we get to the hospital?"

"I'll take the car. Don't worry."

"I'm not," I said. "Don't you worry either. I'll be OK." Why do I keep telling them that? I thought. Why am I so worried about them . . . when I'm the one being put in the hospital? Ah, because you, Hiller, don't count. You're supposed to make them happy, and now you've gone and gotten sick. But I didn't do it on purpose! I thought. I was trying to make *myself* happy! Even if I have to starve to death to do it . . . doesn't make sense, you're not making sense. Per usual, Hiller. You say one thing, then you say another. Rhymes with mother. Mother, me, we, are, one, none, good-bye, Leslie. If you can't have it all, don't have any. I fell asleep to the sound of silverware coming from the dining room. I didn't hear any voices at all.

Mom pulled the curtain around my bed as I undressed. I took off my jeans, looking at my thighs curiously. They weren't there. Mom took one look at me and winced, averting her eyes. I put on my pajamas and sat on the bed uncertainly.

"Just in time for lunch!" a nurse said cheerfully as Mom drew the curtain back. Cheers. What timing.

"Daddy and I are going to the cafeteria for a while, OK?"

"Oh. But you'll come back . . . ?"

"We'll come back in a little while, darling. Here, let me raise your bed so you'll be more comfortable," she said, cranking something at the bottom as the top half of the bed rose, easy-chair style.

"Hey, wow!" I said. "That's neat. All beds should be like this, huh?" She didn't smile. Come on, Mom, I'm not *dead*. "OK, I'll see you later."

I lay in bed, looking at my surroundings with interest. Above the bed was a dim violet lamp, a blood pressure machine, a nurses' call button, an oxygen outlet. My bed was next to the window, and I could see the East River if I sat up all the way. There were four beds in the room, including mine, one of which was free; just as I was wondering where the other occupants were, two women walked in. One was about twenty-five, wearing a long purple nightshirt with a picture of Felix the Cat on the front; the other was about sixty, and she was wheeling an IV pole.

"Hello," she said in a friendly voice, climbing onto the bed next to mine and pulling her tray over to the bed.

"Hi."

"Hi," the younger woman said. "My name is Karen."

"Hi, mine's Leslie."

"Stella Brodkin," the other one said, nodding and then lifting the silver dome off her plate. "Mm, chicken."

"My doctor told me everyone here is on a special diet or something?" I said.

"Well, some of the patients are," Karen said. "I think

they put people here when they don't know what's wrong with them, in case maybe it's something in their diet, so they can keep track. They put me here because they didn't know where else to put me."

"What's wrong with you?"

"I have a collapsed lung." She rolled her eyes. "Wouldn't you know it, the day my boyfriend comes to visit from Michigan, I get put in the hospital."

"What caused it?" I said.

"They don't know. But it's reinflating—they think I can go home on Wednesday."

"What are you in for, Mrs. Brodkin?" I said.

"The craziest thing—I went to the dentist because my gums were bleeding, and wham, here I am."

"Really?" I said. "That *is* strange. What do they think it is?"

She threw her hands up. "You think they tell me anything? God forbid. They're taking tests, and I'm waiting to hear. It better be good—they've taken so much blood they're running out of veins to hit." She pushed back her sleeves, showing me the bruises on the insides of her elbows. They were every color of the rainbow. "Aren't you going to have lunch?"

"I'm not hungry." I paused, then said, "That's why I'm here. I went on a diet and lost too much weight."

"I wish I had your problem!" Karen said, laughing.

"No, you don't," I replied in a toneless voice.

"Well—for two weeks anyway."

The rest of that day was a blur: nurses, interns, questions, a million questions. Mom and Dad left when the dinner trays came, at about five, and after they were gone, I wandered down to the end of the hall. The solarium was empty; there were two tan vinyl couches, a TV, a pay phone, a few ashtrays. I wandered back to my room, stopping in the bathroom on the way. Pee into a tin pitcher, don't forget, so they can measure it. "Hiller" was scrawled on the outside. Wow, my very own private pitcher. "And when you have a bowel movement, write the time under your name on the chart," they'd told me. It won't take them long to read it, I thought. Oh, brother. What a way to live.

After taking my blood pressure, temperature, and pulse for what seemed like the twentieth time, a nurse handed me a clear orange pill. "It'll help you sleep," she said. "Some people have trouble sleeping their first night in a hospital." I may as well, I thought, taking it. Mrs. Brodkin probably snores. Within twenty minutes I was out.

"Wake up, dear, time to get weighed."

I opened my eyes; the sun was red as a cherry, rising over the river.

"You're kidding," I mumbled. "What time is it?"

"Ten minutes to six."

"In the *morning?*" I said.

The nurse laughed. "Come on, dearie, everybody has to get weighed. Take off your nightclothes, and put this on." She handed me a heavy white robe.

Everyone on the floor was lined up in the hall in a white robe, and one after another we were weighed. I was the youngest one there, except for a boy who looked about nine or ten. There was something strange about the way he looked—his stomach was swollen out like a Biafran's, but the rest of him looked fine.

"Hi, I'm Andy," he said in a low voice.

"I'm tired," I responded, and he laughed. "Leslie."

"How old are you?"

"I'll be fifteen in August."

"I'm fifteen," he said. "I look a lot younger, I know. I have this liver problem, and it stunted my growth. But there's a new serum they're going to try on me. A doctor in Florida is testing it."

"*Next,*" the nurse said, looking at me impatiently.

"Oh, sorry," I said, getting on the scale. It said 34.6 kilos. How can I weigh the same as I did yesterday? I thought, beginning to get upset. Was that pill a trick?

"34.6, minus .4. 34.2," the nurse said. I looked at her questioningly. "The robe weighs .4."

After the nurse who woke me up, the nice one, took my vital signs, I went back to sleep and was reawakened by the arrival of the breakfast trays.

"Uhh," I moaned. "How's a person supposed to get any rest around here?"

Just after the trays were taken away, a bunch of interns, maybe six of them, flocked in, gathering around Karen's bed.

"Don't worry," Mrs. Brodkin said, seeing my expression. "They're just making rounds. They come every morning."

"What do they do?"

"They ask questions; they take blood; then they ask more questions. You ask *them* a question, they give you an answer it would take Einstein to figure out what it means," she grumbled good-naturedly.

"I can't get a vein." The intern turned around nervously, and another one came over to confirm it. It was my third morning there.

"Did you try the other arm?"

"It's worse than this one." They removed the rubber thing they'd tied around my upper arm. "OK, we're going to have to go to the femoral artery."

"The what?" I said.

"Can you pull down your pants? Just a little—that's fine." He rubbed some alcohol on the inside top of my thigh.

"You're going to ruin my bikini line," I joked. He stuck the needle in, and I bit my hand.

Later on Dr. Lese came. With him was a dark-haired woman, wearing a white coat over a tweed suit.

"This is Dr. Sussman," he said.

"Nice to meet you," she said to me, holding out her hand. I don't like her smile, I thought. Supercilious. Come on, Les, give her a chance.

"Dr. Lese says you know what's wrong with me," I said.

"Yes, well, from everything he's told me, it sounds to me as if you have anorexia nervosa."

"Ano—what?" I said. Boy, I must sound like a real idiot these days.

"Anorexia nervosa. It's Latin; it means 'nervous loss of appetite.' "

"Oh," I said. "But I didn't really *lose* my appetite . . ." I faltered.

"Yes, well, it's not a very accurate name for the illness." She turned to Dr. Lese. "What is she being given now?"

"I've had her on Valium, twenty."

"I want her on Stelazine," Dr. Sussman said briskly. She looked over at me appraisingly. "We can start with twenty, and then we'll see."

So, I thought. I'm getting a new tranquilizer, and I have an illness that has a name.

"You mean there are other people who've done what I've done?" I said.

"Yes, it appears to be on the rise. I've seen only one case of it myself," she said, pursing her lips. "Come, let's find a place where we can talk." Dr. Lese waved at us and left, white coat flying. We went down the hall and into the empty conference room.

"What's Stelazine?" I said, sitting down across from her.

"It's a neuroleptic drug I use with many of my patients, with great success," she said. "It will make you less anxious, so that you can start gaining some of that weight back."

"I don't *want* to gain any weight!" I said loudly. My lip began to tremble.

"Why don't you tell me about it?" she said, and I burst into tears.

Stop it, Hiller, you look like a complete idiot! "I'm sorry," I said, wiping my eyes. She handed me a Kleenex. "I worked so hard for this, and now you're telling me to give it up. I can't. I won't."

"I'm sorry to see you so unhappy. But you must begin eating, or we'll have to tube-feed you, Leslie. You can't continue to lose weight." Oh, no? Somebody, help. Help me.

"This Stelazine, it won't have any effect on my metabolism, will it?"

"No, it will just make you less anxious, so that we can begin trying to understand what's bothering you."

"I know what's bothering me—I feel fat."

"But that isn't true. You're not fat. You're emaciated." What are you doing, lady? I know I'm not fat. I said I *feel* fat. "Your fear of gaining weight is irrational; it has nothing to do with the facts."

"Even if you're right, that doesn't make it any less scary," I shot back.

"No, it doesn't. Tell me, did your mother make a big deal about eating?"

"Yeah . . . but no more than any other neurotic Jewish mother I know," I said. "Anyway, I know shrinks always blame the mother when the kid has problems, but I love my mother. I really do." I paused, then said, "Do you believe me?"

"Of course, I believe what you tell me," she said. "Our time is up now, Leslie." That surprised me; we'd only

105

been in there for about twenty minutes. She got up, and I followed her. "I'll be back to see you on Friday."

"Not till Friday?" I said, trying to hide my dismay.

"No. I'm sorry, this is a very bad week for me." Hey, what a coincidence, doc—it's kind of an off week for me, too. ". . . want you to start eating a little," she was saying. "If you lose any more weight by the end of the week, we'll have to begin tube feedings."

I felt peaceful, skimming in and out of consciousness; a kind of submissive peace. Take me, Stelazine, I'm all yours. Every morning I sat on the radiator, using my robe for a cushion, watching the nurse change the bed linen. She'd toss the sheet up, and it would billow out, then float down slowly, like a parachute, the scent of detergent mingling with the heat. And she'd chatter away in her Irish singsong, not expecting me to listen, and her voice became a melody dancing on the bars of the morning sunlight. I'd pretend I was four years old, home from school getting over a cold; Lucy, the housekeeper, was making my bed. Lucy, who always laughed at my jokes . . . and Mom was in the kitchen, making Farina. I won't eat it plain, I'd tell her, and she'd dot the top with Nestlé's chocolate morsels, which melted instantly. Dad is playing the Moonlight Sonata in the studio. Just the three of us, then . . . wait, that can't be right. Where was Hilda? I don't remember her being there at all—just Mom. Don't try to figure it out, Leslie—what does it matter anyhow? Mom, I love you. I wish—

106

After my linen was changed, I'd take a long, steaming hot bath; a nurse would knock after a while to see if I was all right, and I'd ease myself out of the tub slowly so I wouldn't faint. The water was so hot I barely needed a towel. And I'd put on my pajamas and go back to bed, back to sleep.

Get well cards began coming; Judy came to visit, bringing an African violet plant, which I put on the radiator by mistake, and it died overnight. A card came from Robin, saying she was afraid to visit me, that it would be too painful, and she hoped I'd understand.

I tried to eat an egg white, a piece of tomato, safe things—I spit them out into a napkin, leaving the napkin on the tray. I don't want to lie anymore. What's the difference? They're going to let me die anyway. The nurses were gentle with me; they didn't know what to make of me. Do you want something that isn't on the menu? Ice cream? Strawberries? Eighteen dollars a pound? We'll fly them in . . . isn't there anything? Yes, but it's a secret—I want everything, everything! *Shhh*—don't tell them. Because you can't explain the rules to them. They don't understand. Don't even think about what you want because it's hopeless, don't you know that? I was down to seventy-three pounds.

"Leslie?" Mom said when she arrived on Thursday afternoon. "What's the matter?"

"Huh?"

"You look dopey."

"Mom, this stuff they're making me take, I don't like

it," I said, trying not to slur as I spoke. "I don't know about Dr. Sussman. I don't know if she knows what she's doing."

"I know. Leslie, Daddy and I called the Higginses. You remember them?"

I nodded. We'd rented their house in Brewster before we bought ours.

"They're both psychiatrists, and they've told us about two doctors who specialize in treating anorexia nervosa. They've been treating it for years, and they're supposed to be the best in the field."

"Two?" I said sleepily. I know I'm excited, I thought. I know I am, but these pills don't let me feel. "Mom, can I see them? Please?"

"We're calling them today. One is a pediatrician who specializes in treating anorexia, a Dr. Gold. And Dr. Wilcox is a psychiatrist."

"A woman?"

Mom nodded. "They have a program at Columbia Presbyterian Hospital. It might mean being there for three or four months."

"Three or four *months?*" I repeated slowly.

"That's what the Higginses said, but we haven't spoken to Dr. Gold yet—"

"I don't care, Mom," I interrupted. "If they're good, I don't care how long I have to be there. But the money—"

"Stop it. Money has nothing to do with it," she said firmly. "We have insurance, and after it runs out, we have other resources, and we'll manage. We're not poor.

We won't starve. . . ." I laughed, and she shifted nervously. "One doesn't try to save money on doctors. Your health is all that matters."

"Thank you," I said. "Thank you, Mom."

She reached over and squeezed my hand. "You should only be well," she whispered fervently. "That's all I want —for you to be well again." Go away, Mom—you're choking me. Being well doesn't just mean eating—it means something else, too. I don't know what. But you wouldn't like it, Mom. I know. Don't go! Please, I didn't mean it. I didn't.

"Mommy? Remember the note I wrote you? The heart?"

"Yes—"

"Do you still have it?"

"Of course I do. I treasure it," she said.

"Good. Because it's all true, what I said."

"Yes, darling—I know it is," she said, her eyes filling with tears. "My darling Leslie—I love you so very much!"

Cavett came to visit me that evening. She felt awkward at first, but after a while she loosened up. Annie broke up with her boyfriend; Marla's contact lenses fell down the drain in the bathroom; there was a dance at Trinity that Saturday night, but she was afraid to go alone.

"I feel so trivial," she said suddenly. "I mean, here you are in a hospital bed and I'm telling you these stupid things. . . ."

"They're *not* stupid—don't stop, please? I *want* to hear."

She shrugged self-consciously. "They told everyone about you in homeroom yesterday, and everyone's been asking me about you."

"What do you tell them?"

"That you're in here, and that they're trying to find out what's wrong with you."

"I found out the name of what I have," I said. "It's called anorexia nervosa."

"Anorexia nervosa?"

"It's Latin for nervous loss of appetite. I don't know why they call it that because it isn't true."

Cavett looked pensive. "You know," she said, "I think—there was a girl in my old school—she was a few grades ahead of me, so I didn't know her, but I remember now—"

"Well, what?"

"That must be what she had," she said, staring into space. "She got thinner and thinner and thinner till she looked like someone in a concentration camp. . . ."

Maybe I should drop Leslie and go by my middle name, I thought idly. "What happened to her?"

"She—she went off to some hospital," Cavett said, and began going through her purse. "I hope I have change for the bus."

"But did she get better?" I pressed. "Cavett, look at me!"

She bit her lip nervously. "Hey, Leslie, I'm sorry. I shouldn't have brought it up."

"Cavett—"

"She died." I stared at her, stunned. "Look, maybe she didn't have anorexia at all. Maybe she had cancer or something. I don't *know*."

"It's OK," I said. "Hey, listen, let's talk about something else. Tell me about Annie. How come they broke up?"

We sat around for a while longer in the solarium, and I told her about Gold and Wilcox. Andy asked us to play one round of gin with him (he won), and then it was eight, and visiting hours were over. Cavett walked back to my bed with me to get her coat. The curtain around Mrs. Brodkin's bed was drawn all the way, and I heard her husband's voice.

"Who's in there?" Cavett whispered.

"Mrs. Brodkin. She's *really* nice. It's so awful—she was put in here by her dentist, if you can believe that, because her gums were bleeding, right? And it turns out she has leukemia."

"Gosh," Cavett said. "Gosh, how old is she?"

"Sixty-two. That's not old, Cavett. That's so young to be dying." And I'm fourteen and a half, I thought.

"Gosh."

"Well. Now that I've cheered you up," I said sarcastically, and we smiled at each other in relief. "Thanks a lot for coming—I really appreciate it."

"I'd have come sooner, but I didn't know if you wanted to see anyone. When you find out about these other doctors, will you call me? If you feel like it, that is. I can always call your mom myself," she added hastily.

"Sure I'll call you! Hey, don't *you* start acting weird around me. You're my salvation."

"Yeah, some salvation," she said, shaking her head. "Well—feel better." She hesitated, then quickly kissed my cheek. "OK?" She waved, and I waved back.

The next morning Mom and Dad arrived at nine-thirty.

"Come on, get dressed. You're getting out of here," Dad said, sounding the closest to cheerful I'd heard him sound in ages.

"Hey, what's going on?" I said, sitting up.

"You have an appointment with Dr. Gold at eleven, and if he confirms the diagnosis, there's a bed available this afternoon."

"What about Dr. Sussman?"

"We called her yesterday," Mom said.

"I didn't like her at all," said Dad.

"All right, Max, it's not important now," Mom said, gathering my things. "Why don't you wait in the hall so Leslie can get dressed?" Hang onto your jeans, Hiller We're going to have another go.

CHAPTER NINE

We arrived at Columbia Presbyterian at two and took the elevator up to the eleventh floor of Babies' Hospital, as Dr. Gold had instructed. He'd be stopping by to look in on me that afternoon. Mom and Dad walked into the nurses' station while I lagged behind, looking around. To the left was a kind of sitting room for visitors, painted hospital green. I peered in and saw one pay phone and orange couches along two of the walls.

Then a nurse came and led us down a long corridor toward what I thought would be the solarium. Instead, we walked into a large room with eight beds, each in its own green-curtained cubicle. I followed her to one of the corner cubes; there was a label on the end of the bed which read: "Leslie Hiller, Dr. Gold, 14 yrs." I noticed labels on two other beds on my side of the room; one said, "Jessica Marks, Dr. Gold, 16 yrs.," the other, "Carrie Friedman, Dr. Gold, 12 yrs."

I was given a pair of striped hospital pajamas, and I

113

put them on, checking to make sure my ribs were still sticking out. I heard the nurse talking and listened through the curtains for a moment.

"No, she doesn't need anything."

"A toothbrush?"

"Toothbrush, hairbrush, pajamas, robe, the hospital will provide everything she needs. Those are Dr. Gold's rules."

I wandered out of my cube, looking down at myself and then at Mom. I wondered if she was thinking what I was: that I looked like an inmate at Auschwitz. Just then an emaciated girl came out of the solarium behind the ward. I looked past her briefly and saw that there was an upright piano there.

"Hi!" she said brightly. "I'm Jessica. Are you Leslie?"

I nodded. "God, you're skinny. I'd give anything to look like you." Her face closed, though her smile remained. Suddenly another girl came up behind her. She was very small, maybe four feet eleven, and her face was drawn, but I could tell she was really quite beautiful.

"Hi, I'm Carrie."

"Do you have—" She nodded. "You're so young."

"I'm not really that young," she said, looking hurt.

I couldn't take my eyes off her. "I'm sorry if I'm staring; it's just that I thought I was the only one in the world."

"So did I. Now there's three of us up here. I just came a week ago. One girl went home yesterday."

"Was she better?" I said, searching her face. Mom and Dad walked over then.

"Leslie, we have to go now," Dad said gently. "They won't let us stay." He gave me a quick hug. "You take care of yourself."

Then Mom hugged me, and I watched them walk back up the long corridor and turn, vanishing.

An hour later Dr. Gold came and took me to an empty room. We sat across from each other, and I looked at him expectantly.

"OK, Leslie, I'm going to explain the rules," he said, as though talking to a young child. "We do not make our patients eat, but you *must* drink five glasses of fluids a day."

"Or?"

"Or we'll put you on an IV."

"OK," I said. "I'll drink water."

"Not water. It has to be calorie liquids. Milk, juice, soda—"

"No," I interrupted. "I won't do it."

"That's entirely up to you. It's either that or the IV," he said calmly. "As I said, we don't make our patients eat, but I'll tell you this—you won't get out of here till you're eating everything on your tray. So if you're *smart*, you'll eat whatever's put in front of you."

Don't bother arguing, Hiller. They can't make you do anything. "Do we get menus?"

"No, you get the standard meal being served that day." He grinned at me. "When you get out of here, you can choose what you eat. Here, you eat what's put in front of you. Got it?"

"What about visitors?"

"Only your parents, once a week. Also, no sending or receiving mail, and you're allowed one phone call a day. To your parents." He went on to tell me that I'd be spending my first week having a battery of tests done, having absolutely every conceivable part of me checked out, and that Dr. Wilcox would see me four times a week.

"And when you go to the bathroom—"

"I know, save it," I said.

"Right. Now, any questions?"

I thought for a minute. "The other kids up here have normal things wrong with them, right? I mean, they're not crazy like us."

"This is not a psychiatric ward, if that's what you mean," he said.

"And I suppose you have reasons for all these rules?" I said.

He looked faintly amused, and said, "You are sick, are you not?" I nodded. "We are removing you completely from the environment in which you became ill."

The man makes sense, I thought. Now, can you change the insides, too?

"It's sugar water in the IV anyway," Carrie said. "You might as well drink."

I was lying on my bed, unable to move. Carrie was sitting on the end of it. "I guess. It probably has as many calories," I reasoned, calculating in my head. No matter

116

how you cut it, I'll be taking in 500 calories a day, and there's no way out. This is it, kid.

"How long have you been doing this?"

"Since Christmas." We began exchanging stories, and the more we talked, the funnier it all sounded.

"I dropped food into the piano," Carrie said. "My parents took me to the doctor after three weeks. I think they noticed the piano smelled funny."

"Did you throw up?"

"No. Lisa, the girl who left, she did that. I took Ex-Lax. It doesn't really make you lose weight—"

"I bet it makes you feel empty, though," I said enviously. She nodded. "I don't think Jessica likes me."

"Nah, she's just like that. She never talks about her problems."

Just then a nurse's aide came over to the bed. Her pin said "Miss Miller."

"OK, juice cart is here. Come on, you two. Carrie, you've got 800 cc's left. Got a long way to go, tootsie pie!"

We got up and walked over to the cart, where Jessica was dutifully downing a glass of apple juice.

"Orange juice," Carrie said in a tired voice.

"I'll have ginger ale." Here goes nothing, Hiller. I drank it quickly and glanced over toward the window. Carrie had just poured half her juice down the sink. I turned back and put down my cup. Then I went to my bed, climbed in, and buried my face against the scratchy pillowcase.

According to rules, we had to sit in front of our trays whether we ate or not. On Monday morning Carrie, Jessica, and I were sitting at the small round table at the other end of the ward, trying to deal with breakfast. Carrie pushed her food around with her fork, staring at it intently. Jessica carefully scraped the butter off her toast, then ate only the crusts. Then, to my amazement, she ate her scrambled eggs. I was staring at my cornflakes when Dr. Gold came into the ward, followed by a tall woman in a black lambskin coat, the kind Mom wore when I was very young. She walked with dignity and purpose.

"Leslie, this is Dr. Wilcox," Dr. Gold said. I got up and walked toward her, and we shook hands.

"I can see someone else first if you're still having breakfast," she said.

"No, I'm finished," I said wryly.

"Sure?" She glanced over my shoulder at the table. "OK."

I followed her, trying to run a little to keep pace. She looked over at me and slowed down. We took the elevator down to seven, and she took me into a small room with a table and two chairs, and we sat down. She smiled at me briefly; then her face became serious. She pushed her glasses back into place.

"So. Why don't you begin by telling me when all this started?"

I'm less and less sure I know when it was, I thought, but dismissed it and began with the Christmas flu. When

I'd come up to the present, I stopped, then said, "I thought when I got thin, everything would be—"

"Perfect."

"Yes," I said, surprised. "How did you know?" She just looked at me. "And I thought everything else in my life already was."

"Like what, for instance?"

"Well . . . I got along with my mother . . ." How can I explain it all? I thought. What did Mom say in her letter to me? I rattled off the lists of good grades, talents, all the things that made the dictator shout: Spoiled brat, what right do you have to mess up the Hiller Harmony by getting sick?

"But this diet gave me a sense of—*power*."

"Power over what?"

"Myself!"

"Yeah? Who else?"

I stared at her. "Well, who?"

"You tell me."

I threw my hands up. "How should I know? If I knew, I wouldn't need a psychiatrist!"

"I don't have the answers for you, Leslie. My job is to help you find them within yourself. You come to me and say, 'How should I know?' I can't tell you how you feel." I looked down at my feet. "You sure had Mom and Pop hopping around in hysterics."

"I never wanted to hurt them!" She looked at me skeptically. "I didn't! I wanted to be thin!"

"Eating is not your problem, Leslie. It never was; it never will be." Now it was my turn to look skeptical.

"You fill your head up with this eating nonsense so you won't have to face the real problems, but starving doesn't get rid of them."

"Well," I said, not knowing what else to say. "But if I keep on losing—"

"You'll die." Like Cavett's friend, I thought. How nice. "How thin do you have to be to realize that starving will never make you happy? Look at yourself!"

I do look at myself, all the time, every day, and I hate it. Don't you see how much I hate it? What would it take to make you do this, how scared would you have to be? Suppose someone said, "If you don't starve, your mother will be killed." Imagine it. That's not why I do it, of course, but just imagine it. If you eat, she'll die. And if your mother dies, you die. I would. Eating = greedy = selfish, and selfish is dangerous. Leslie never asks for things. If I were selfish, Mom wouldn't love me. But the funny thing is . . . Mom pretends to be so selfless, yet manages to suck me dry till I don't even feel like a person. Till I can't tell us apart.

Hey, Mom, are you afraid that if you're selfish outright, and choose to live, you'll lose the people you love, who love you—like me? The way Margolee would have lost her mother if she'd chosen to go to the right? . . . I know, I know how you feel, because I feel that way, too. I know my starving is partly selfishness in disguise. You told me that Margolee couldn't let her mother face the gas chamber alone, and that's why she went with her. But don't you see that's only *half* the truth? Don't you see that Margolee needed to have her mother keep on

120

thinking what a wonderful, selfless daughter she had—and that's why she's DEAD?

And tell me, Wilcox, could you ever understand? And if you were able to, could it ever make any difference? Can you, can anyone restore Leslie Margolee Hiller, royal convoluted wacked-out Leslie, Leslie, Leslie, please, Leslie, I love you so much, I thought, hearing a new voice in my head. But not really new; just so old, it sounded new. I love you—I *love* you—hey, it's me, *Leslie*, talking to you, *Leslie*, in a rare guest appearance. Dr. Wilcox held out a Kleenex, and I took it from her.

"Why are you crying, Leslie?" she said gently.

"Because I looked at myself. I did what I was told, which is what always gets me into trouble!" I answered, and began laughing and crying at the same time.

"And what did you see?" I became silent. "Was it so terrible?"

"Half," I said, then paused, sniffling. "Can you help me?" She handed me another Kleenex, and I laughed again. "Thanks a lot. You charge for these, too?"

"Double for the scented ones."

Then I began telling her about it.

After the first week it seemed I'd been there forever. Mornings, except for Wednesdays, Wilcox came; Gold came every day. Afternoons were spent in the playroom on the seventh floor. There was a woodwork shop with an electric saw, clay, paints, you name it. And a small library, where Carrie and I often sat, talking and listening to her transistor radio. (It was absolutely contraband, but we'd wheedled Miss Miller into lending it to us.) We read the *Merck Manual* aloud to each other, deciding we had every disease in it.

In the evenings we watched TV occasionally, but more often than that I played the piano and we sang. I can play by ear, not fantastically but well enough, and the other kids on the floor began coming in to listen and sing with us. Which made me feel great. We sang everything: folk songs, songs from musicals—even Jessica laughed the first time I played "I got plenty o' nothin', and nothin's plenty for me!"—television commercials. "Whaddya want when ya gotta have somethin', and it's gotta be sweet, and it's gotta be a lot, and ya gotta have it *now?*" we belted. Those were moments when I liked myself.

Miss Miller had to cut out a little chunk of hair for me because the idiot who gave me the electroencephalogram got glue all over my hair, and it wouldn't come out, no matter how much I scrubbed and combed. The GI series was the worst, I guess—well, the IVP, where they injected a dye so they could X-ray my kidneys, wasn't too far behind. It was all like leaving your body to science and living to see it happen, but I didn't mind. I'd stopped feeling like a freak. I have a bona fide illness, and they're checking me out. And I'm a little bit more Leslie-ish. Just a little.

"Hey, the new one's here," Carrie said one morning, poking her head into the solarium.

"You're kidding," I said, standing up. "How bad is she?"

"Where?" Jessica called.

"She's in a room down the hall," Carrie said as I entered the ward. "They're moving her in here tomorrow."

"Have you seen her?" I said.

"Nah, Gold was in there. He's gone now, though."

"Should we go say hello?" Jessica said.

"Yeah, let's go," I replied. "She was in Sinai Psychiatric."

"How'd you know?" Carrie said as the three of us walked down the hall.

"Grapevine," I said, grinning. Carrie stopped in front of a half-open door and pointed, and we all looked at each other. Finally I stuck my head into the room and saw a heavyset woman standing next to the bed with her back to us.

"Uh . . . hi, are you Mrs. Balser?" I said timidly. The woman turned around quickly, her face full of fear. I smiled at her, thinking: Look normal, Hiller, she's spooked out.

"Yes?" she said, as though she weren't sure at all.

"Hi, I'm Leslie Hiller. I—we're Dr. Gold's patients, too."

"Oh, yes. Hello. It's nice to meet you," she said, trying to smile.

"Hi, Nicole," I said, and looked at the girl in the bed. Skinny, I thought; not horrendous, though. Has a face like mine—not gaunt, never will be. She had short dark hair and bangs, and her eyes looked glassy, as though they couldn't quite focus on anything. Carrie and Jessica came in and stood beside me, introducing themselves.

"Hi," Nicole said, looking utterly dazed.

"You'll be in the ward with us tomorrow," I said, trying to sound cheerful.

"Dr. Gold told me," she said, in a voice barely above a whisper. "I'm sorry, I'm really tired. . . ." I looked at Jessica and then at Mrs. Balser.

"She's tired," Mrs. Balser repeated softly. "She's been under sedation. . . ."

Of course, I thought. Like I was. They drug you up and pretend it's for your sake when really it's just that they don't want to have to listen to you.

"Stelazine?" I murmured.

"Thorazine."

"Don't worry, they don't use any of that here."

"Thank you," she said, her eyes filled with tears.

"We even have fun here sometimes," I said, looking over in desperation at Carrie and Jessica.

"Well . . ." Mrs. Balser said doubtfully. I reached over impulsively and squeezed her shoulders. "Thank you so much—thank you for coming to say hello—"

"Thank you," Nicole echoed. "I'm sorry, I can't really—"

"It's OK, we'll see you later."

"You'll all get better," Mrs. Balser said, and I nodded, following Carrie and Jessica out. We will, sure we will. A magic doctor will go zap, and we'll be well.

"She's weird," Carrie said as we made our way back to the ward.

"How can you tell? She's so zonked on Thorazine, you can't tell a thing," I replied, hopping on a laundry cart and careening wildly down the hall, narrowly missing Miss Miller as she grabbed the juice cart out of the way.

"Hiller!" she yelled. "Off the cart!"

"Shhh," I said, putting my index finger to my lips. "This is a *hospital*."

"Very funny. You've been told not to ride up and down the halls on the cart. Now I'll have to put it in your report." I bowed apologetically. Miss Miller grumbled and checked her cart. "And you better start drinking, too. You've got 600 cc's to go, and if you don't get going soon . . ."

"You'll stick an IV in my arm," I finished for her. "Then I could ride the IV pole. Not bad, huh?"

"I'm not fooling, now . . ."

"Oh, all right, all *right*. Ginger ale."

She filled my cup, and I started walking onto the ward. "Ah-ah-ah—drink it *here*," Miller said. I pivoted and drank without stopping.

"OK?" I said.

She grunted. "OK, Carrie, you're next. What'll it be?"

"I'm not thirsty," Carrie whined.

"I'm warning you, Carrie . . ."

"Coke," Carrie whispered.

I went off into the solarium and stood by the window overlooking the hospital garden. Spring had arrived. Winter's gone and another season has come in its place; I'm eating a little, enough to maintain seventy-one pounds, and Wilcox says things that make sense. But sense has nothing to do with it, I thought. Nothing at all. It would have been better to let me die, because the hell never stops, the dictator never eases up. It's all well and good while we're in here, and when we eat, we can blame Gold and his rules. But are any of us changing? Jessica's gaining weight. I might, too. Someday. I'll lose it again, though. You'll see, Wilcox. My way *does* work. It does— it's only that I didn't get thin enough. Maybe if I got to be sixty pounds, maybe then I'd be happy. You can't tell me it isn't true—I don't believe you.

I wonder what Sammy thinks of all this, I thought. I wonder what they've told him. They probably think they can keep telling him, "Leslie went overboard on her diet," just because he's eight, but I know better. Why do people think kids can be lied to? Maybe Sammy won't be like me, though. Maybe he'll ask things he isn't supposed to ask. Not like old Leslie-keep-the-peace Hiller, who always plays the game.

Don't ask Mom about sex, she'll get embarrassed. Don't tell her if I'm less than thrilled with the present she gave me, she'll be disappointed. Don't tell her I'm sad/mad as hell because she didn't get rid of Hilda, "because you know she would have, if they'd had more money," says the dictator. Don't tell her she doesn't *want* me to stay and listen to Dad play the piano once she's home, she *means* to interrupt, so I keep my distance from him, refuse his emotional invitations. Mom, she won't take no to an invitation. She shuts you out if you say, "No, I won't play. I *won't* beg you to please, please not buy me expensive clothes and then announce your own hideous three-dollar bargain purchase in the same breath. Nor will I beg you to take the pills you're supposed to take, stop making dips for every party on the West Side, and then comfort you when you cry because you're so tired and everyone expects so much of you. Nor will I tell you you're the best mother in the world because there isn't any such thing, there's no standard measuring cup in your kitchen in which to test whether you're falling short of Best-Mothering." . . . Mom, it's my fault, too, because I play it with you. Together we make a stereo, different sounds coming from each speaker, mingling, playing a single tune. And it's not enough to turn it *off* because we're supposed to be two different records. Won't you listen to my singing? I'm so afraid to take the chance!

Shhh, Leslie—Mom doesn't know what's wrong with you, none of them do. She's kidding herself—she wouldn't mind at all if I were anorexic, if only I'd eat a little! The only thing separating us is fifty-five pounds. And it's the only thing that can keep us together.

One morning a week later I was playing solitaire on my bed.

"*Hey*, Gab! How're you doing?" Jessica said suddenly, coming out of her cubicle. I leaned over to see a girl

127

entering the ward with Miss Miller. I looked over at the empty bed; the tag on the end said, "Gabriella Small, Dr. White, 8 yrs."

"Great! See my new frog?" Gabby said, holding up a large stuffed green creature.

"Boy, pretty soon you'll have the biggest frog collection in the country," Jessica said.

"The *country?*" Gabby replied indignantly. "The *world*, you mean. Right, Miss Miller?" Her eyes were the clearest aquarium blue I'd ever seen, her cheeks like McIntosh apples, her short, straight hair honey gold. I couldn't take my eyes off her. She sparkled.

"Right, Gab," Miss Miller said. "Ready to get undressed? You need help?"

"Of course not," she said, and began to unbutton her shirt. Miss Miller drew the curtain to her cubicle.

"Hey, Jessica," I whispered. "How do you know her?"

"She's been here before," Jessica replied, turning away.

"Oh," I said, more than a little annoyed. Why is it like pulling teeth asking her anything? "Well, what does she come in for?"

"Blood transfusions."

"Oh," I said again, and gave up.

"Jessica, is Carrie still here?" Gabby called.

"Yeah, she'll be back in a little while," Jessica called back.

"Oh, *good*," Gabby said, and I laughed to myself.

"OK, Gab, hold still," I heard Miss Miller say, and then I heard a loud "OUCH!" A minute later Gabby emerged, pushing her IV pole.

"Will you put Henry on my pole?" she said.

"*Who* is *Henry?*" Miss Miller said, putting her hand on her hip.

"My *frog*," Gabby said impatiently. "I brought a string so you can tie him to the bottom, see?"

Miss Miller obliged. "OK, I'm going to get the trays now," she announced. "Henry," she grumbled good-naturedly.

Carrie padded in a moment later, and when she saw Gabby, her face lit up. "Hi, Gabby!"

"Hi! I've been waiting for you. Guess what?"

"What?"

"Eddie's coming to see me tomorrow," Gabby said, smiling radiantly. "He promised to teach me how to play poker, but I'm not supposed to tell Mom and Dad."

"Who's Eddie?" I asked.

"Eddie's my brother, well, *one* of my brothers; see, I have three altogether," Gabby explained, "only one of them's in college, so I *never* get to see him except on Christmas and things like that, and Thanksgiving—"

"Gab-gab-Gabby," Miss Miller joked, pushing in the lunch cart.

"Oh, shhh!" Gabby laughed. "It's not polite to interrupt, Miss Miller. *Anyhow*, Eddie's thirteen, and he wins a lot of money playing poker, only no one's supposed to know or they'll make him put it in the bank for *college*," she said, rolling her eyes. "That's what they make *me* do all the time, whenever I get any money, 'you-have-to-

129

save-it-for-college.' " She made a face and then grinned wickedly. "Only if I win money at poker, nobody will know!"

Suddenly we all burst out laughing, even Jessica and Miss Miller.

"You want to have your lunch at the table with the girls?" Miss Miller said.

"Yes," she said, plopping down and smacking her hand on the chair next to hers. "Carrie's sitting here."

We all sat around doing our peculiar things with our food, but Gabby didn't seem to notice; she just kept talking. Carrie actually talked instead of just staring down at her plate and shoving things back and forth.

"What kind of meat is this?" Gabby said, holding up a string of it.

"I think it's supposed to be London broil," I said, nodding in sympathy.

"Uck." Gabby dropped it and attacked her mashed potatoes with gusto. "Know what we had last night? *Pizza*, boy, it was mmmmm—with *pepperoni*," she added, licking her lips.

A girl wandered into the ward and walked over to our table. She looked about seven or eight and had stringy yellow hair and buckteeth. She kicked at Gabby's frog lightly and then backed away from Gabby's glare.

"I'm having my tonsils out tomorrow, and I'll get all the ice cream I want," she announced, pursing her lips.

"Whoop-de-doo," Carrie muttered, twirling her finger. I laughed.

"So what's so great about that?" Gabby said coolly. "Who wants ice cream all the time?"

"*You* do, I bet," the girl said, batting her eyes. "Ha-ha." Oh, ugh, I thought.

"What's *that?*" she said, pointing at our trays and wrinkling her nose. "I had a roast beef sandwich for lunch."

"Oh, you did, did you?" I said.

"What are you here for?" the girl said to Gabby, ignoring me.

"None of your business," Gabby said.

"I told you what *I'm* here for; now you tell *me*," she persisted. I looked at Jessica, thinking: For once in your life *say* something.

"I told you, none of your business!" Gabby repeated.

"Tell me why you're here!" the girl screeched, and began to chant, "Why are you here? Why are you here? Why, oh, why are you he-*ere!*"

"She—" Jessica began.

"I have leukemia, *OK?*"

I stared at Gabby in horror. She'd gone right back to her mashed potatoes, as though she'd just said, "It's twelve-thirty."

"What's that?" the girl said.

"It's a blood disease," Gabby replied.

"Get out of here," Jessica said, standing up abruptly. "Go back to your room."

"Why should I?" the girl countered, backing away all the same.

"Because I said so. You have your own room. This is our room. And we don't want you in our room, so go back to yours."

"Who says I have to?" the girl said weakly. Jessica took a step toward her, and she darted out.

"What a creep," Carrie said, breaking the awkward silence.

"Yeah. Did you see how she kicked Henry?" Gabby said. She took a big sip of milk and wiped her mouth. "She better not do *that* again."

"Don't worry, Gabby," I said, as if in a dream. "If she bugs you, you just yell." I looked at Jessica, questioning. She wouldn't meet my gaze.

"Well, *I'm* done," Gabby said, standing up. "I'm going to ask when we go to the playroom." She wheeled her IV pole out of the ward.

"Jessica?" I said hesitantly.

"What?"

"She looks so healthy." Jessica stared at me dully. "She knows she has leukemia, but she's saving up for college?" I tried again, desperate to get a response.

"Yeah," Jessica whispered.

"But—but doesn't she watch Marcus Welby or anything?" I said, feeling ridiculous. "Doesn't she *know?*"

"Maybe she knows but doesn't say so," Jessica said, looking the closest to crying I'd ever seen her look.

"Hey, Jess, that was really good, how you got rid of that kid," I said. She smiled almost shyly and then got up and walked into the solarium. Carrie and I sat alone in silence.

"So where's Nicole?" Carrie said finally.

"Um, GI series, I think."

"Yuck."

"You're not kidding," I said, and silence fell again. When I thought I couldn't stand another second of it, I remembered something. I got out of my chair and sat in the one Gabby had been in. "Guess what I got?" I said, looking over her shoulder elaborately to make sure no one was watching.

"What?" Carrie said curiously. I stuck my hand into my robe pocket and withdrew it, revealing four half-smoked cigarettes. "Wilcox never finishes them in my sessions." I giggled. "Do you think it's significant?"

Carrie's face became one long grin. "You're not going to believe this," she said. She reached into her pocket to retrieve two stamped-out butts, with only a puff or two left in each. I looked at them and began to choke. "The point is, which one of us is worse?" she said, and we collapsed in hysterics.

"Oh, *God*, we're delinquents," I said when I caught my breath. "Babies' Hospital delinquents." We smiled at each other conspiringly. "Tonight on the back stairs."

She nodded. "Right."

"Carrie?"

"What?"

"It's so unfair," I said softly. "It's so unfair that Gabby's going to die."

"I know," she said, picking up a piece of meat and throwing it back at her plate. "I know."

CHAPTER TEN

At the end of April a new girl came, all sixty-five pounds of her thrashing and screaming like a lunatic. It took three nurses to hold her down. .

"Hey, Nikki," I said, running into her cubicle. "Who the hell is that? Gold didn't say a new one was coming."

"She's got a different doctor," Nicole said. "I heard them talking last night—she was in Psychiatric before, but they didn't know what to do with her."

I walked out casually to look at her bed tag. It said, "Delilah Costello, Dr. Denton, 14 yrs." She was sitting on her bed, and her mother was stroking her hand as she wept. Mrs. Costello turned and gave me a dirty look, and I shot back into Nicole's cube.

"She's an embarrassment!" I whispered.

"I know, she's really buggy, huh?"

Delilah's arrival ended any hopes of having an uninterrupted night's sleep, which was hard to come by to begin with; she was given to wandering about the hospital grounds in the wee hours, sending the night shift into fits of cursing. At first they were panic-stricken, certain they'd be jailed when Delilah was found dead in a gutter on Upper Broadway; but security always found her somewhere in the hospital, which stretched all the way down to the river. There were at least ten different buildings connected to each other by underground tunnels, at least half of which the Gold-Wilcox crew had been through during test week. Sometimes it took up to two hours before they found Delilah, lost in Urology, or buying and throwing out food at the vending machines, or jogging around Ear Nose & Throat. Thanks to Delilah, the night nurses began checking on all of us, bursting into our cubes in the middle of the night with a flashlight. Delilah was always brought back crying or begging for a cup of ice, which she'd then sit and chew in the dark. Loudly.

"I'm surprised nobody bothers you," I remarked one morning, more than a little irritated. "I mean the night nurse in Urology must notice you're not an eighty-year-old man hooked up to a catheter bag." Although actually, I thought, she doesn't look too far from it.

She shrugged, two bones popping up under her pajama shirt and cracking back into place. "In Psychiatric they look at you funny when you go to the bathroom. Here—" She shrugged again and went back to drinking her tomato juice, glancing up at me with a slight smirk. Dr. Gold's patients weren't allowed to drink tomato juice because it was low in calories, and he knew it was all we'd drink if given the chance.

"Hey. How come you do it?" I said.

"Because," she replied, as though it made all the sense

in the world. I nodded and went to wash up. I suppose it makes as much "sense" as anything else, I thought.

"That Delilah's really nuts," I said to Nicole as we passed at the pitchers.

"I know. She's bad for our image," she replied. Then she laughed, shaking her pitcher in the air. "Damn, I can't wait to be able to flush a toilet!"

Sundays were visiting days, and deceptively pleasant. Jessica and Carrie and Nikki and I never talked about it, but the tension was visible to all of us, and Sunday nights always came with a sense of relief. Mom and Dad talked to me cheerfully about trivia, who wore what to the Passover seders, who in our building was getting divorced, and not to worry, Barrow said I could make up the work I was missing over the summer. Supposedly our schools were to send assignments to our parents every couple of weeks for us to do in the hospital, but none of us got much work done.

"Mom, what do you say when the Simons and everyone call me to baby-sit?" I said one Sunday afternoon. Mom had come alone that day because there wasn't anyone to stay with Sammy.

"I tell them you're away at school," she said shortly.

"Away where?"

"At school."

"*School?*" I said loudly. "All of a sudden in the middle of March I went to boarding school? Are you kidding?"

She looked straight at me and said in a clipped voice, "No, I'm not."

"What about your friends? What about the family?"

"I tell them you went overboard with your diet, which is the truth."

I stared at her long and hard. "Why don't you tell them what I have? Is it so shameful?"

"No, it's not shameful, but the fewer people that know, the better, as far as I'm concerned."

"You're afraid they'll think it's your fault, aren't you?" I said slowly.

"Yes, if you must know," she snapped. "It makes *me* look like a bad mother. OK?"

"You don't give me much credit, do you?" I asked.

"What?" she said, startled. "Of course, I give you credit—" She stopped, and her look turned to anger. "*Credit?* You want credit for *this?*"

"I want credit for *something!*"

"I'm going to get some coffee," she said abruptly, picking up her purse.

My mouth dropped open. "Can't I even argue without your walking out on me?"

"I'm not walking out. I'm just getting some coffee."

Now see what you've done? the dictator said. But I was right—I was *right!* Why is it shameful, Mom, to be ill and unhappy and trying to untangle my cockamamie head so I can fix my out-of-commission, brutalized body, no thanks to you? . . . *No thanks!* shouted the dictator. You ungrateful wretch! You greedy little pig, do you have any idea what this lousy bed you're sitting on is costing her? Not to mention Dr. Gold, Dr. Wilcox, Dr. Sussman, Dr. Lese, Dr. Jenkins, Dr. Chester—and an-

137

guish? At least she's saving on the grocery bills, I thought . . . oh, Leslie, shut up, you're horrible. Yes —yes, I am horrible. Because for all her kookiness, she really, really does love me. Who knows why she turned out the way she did? Hitler? Her mother? Her father? First-grade teacher? The books she's read, movies she's seen, slipping on banana peels, and maybe something she was just plain born with? No credit due anyone else? Mommy, I give *you* credit—can't you give me some, too? You may be my mother, but I'm not your creation . . . shut up, Leslie. Fat seventy-four-pound Leslie, by the way. You better keep a tight rein, in this tight reign. Don't you know when the stove is hot? She won't listen. She won't let you fight. And she loves you, Leslie, and she wants what's best for you. The trouble is . . . the trouble is . . .

When she returned half an hour later, I looked at her cautiously. "It's not your fault I'm sick," I said. "Don't you know that? I'm a person, not just a piece of clay you molded wrong."

"Maybe if I'd been home when you were little," she said, starting to cry.

I put my arm around her. "But you couldn't help having to work," I soothed. "And anyway, *I* remember you being there, and I don't remember Hilda at all. It's quality that counts, right?"

"Oh, I don't know," she said, taking a shredded Kleenex out of her bag. "I don't know anything anymore!"

138

"Mom, does it really matter whose 'fault' it is? I mean what's the point in blaming anyway?"

"I'm not *blaming*, I'm—I don't know," she said again. Well, I do, I thought. You want me to tell you it's not anything you did, and so I will tell you. Anyway, even if you did hurt me, it wasn't on purpose. What a bind. How do you get mad at someone whose intentions are good? There aren't any villains in this—I'm the only one that's cruel on purpose. Does Mom care about me? She says she does, but she doesn't know me; she thinks I'm just like her. So I am. But I'm not. Oh, hell. Will the real Leslie M. Hiller please stand up?

That evening I played the piano, adding "Happy Birthday" to the usual repertoire for Gabby—she was back, and it was her ninth birthday. And you never know . . . Dad's words came back to me in a chilling new context. You never know, do you?

"Now they can change the label on my bed," she announced happily. "Leslie, play 'Let's Go Fly a Kite,' " she commanded, and I did. I played a few Schubert waltzes and some rag, which everyone loved, and then most of the kids were hauled off to bed. Nikki and Carrie and I sat around going through old copies of *Woman's Day*, looking at all the food ads with longing, and our conversation shifted to the nurses: who was the nicest, meanest, prettiest, stupidest.

"I know," Carrie said when we ran out of people to discuss. "Let's tell ghost stories!"

139

"I don't know any," I said.

"That's OK, I do," she said.

"Wait, I'll go ask Jessica if she wants to—maybe she knows some, too."

She did, and she came into the solarium and turned out the light. We all sat in a circle on the floor, and Carrie began. "Once there was a farmer, whose only son drowned when he was only six years old . . ."

"What's that?" I whispered suddenly, grabbing Nikki's wrist. We listened intently, then all burst into giggles.

"It's Delilah chewing ice," Nikki said.

Carrie took a deep breath. "OK. There was this farmer . . ."

Jessica knew the best ones, though, because she'd been a junior counselor at camp the previous summer. At the end of one particularly chilling one we heard the door to the solarium creak. Carrie gasped, and all at once we shrieked, grabbing each other in a tangle of bones. Jessica ran to turn on the light; there was nothing there, only the wind blowing through the half-open window. She turned the light back off, and we began laughing wildly, not noticing Miss Lansing, the night nurse, as she entered the room.

"What the hell is going on in here?" she screamed. We stood up instantly, letting out a few leftover giggles. "God damn it, there are *sick* people here!"

Nicole stepped back, and I felt myself flinch as though I'd been slapped. Carrie and Jessica looked down at the floor.

"I want every one of you in bed right this minute,

140

and I don't want to see any of you up again. You got me?" Jessica nodded, and Miss Lansing stormed out and down the hall.

Nicole turned toward me, her eyes shining in the dark. "Why does she think *we*'re here?" she croaked as two tears streamed down her face.

"They hate us," I said. Carrie kicked at the floor with her foot, and Jessica stared at me, expressionless. "They think we're spoiled brats. What right do we have to be wasting bed space when there are kids like Gabby."

Nicole lifted her hands to her face and cried silently. Carrie and Jessica looked at her and then over at me, shifting uncomfortably. I reached my arm out and touched Nicole's shoulder awkwardly, then dropped it, reaching, instead, for a Kleenex from the box on the piano and handing it to her.

"Thank you," she said, and blew her nose.

"They can all go to hell," I whispered after a moment. We stood together like that in the dark, none of us moving, and when Nicole had finished crying, I said, "Come on, guys, let's go to bed."

I made three marionettes in the playroom, cutting up a pair of hospital pajamas to make their clothes out of, and it caught on. Soon everyone wanted to make them. Miss Sills, who ran the playroom, began hauling in shopping bags full of old newspaper to make papier-mâché. Delilah got caught stealing cookies from a boy's room down the hall while he was out having a spinal tap, and the nurses went on a search rampage in her cubicle. She'd been hoarding food in the most incredible places—food buried in her plants, candy in her flashlight instead of batteries, food in the bedsprings. She also began fooling around with our pee pitchers, dumping them out entirely or pouring all of it into one.

"Well, well!" Miller chirped one day. "Hiller voided 200 cc's of tomato juice!" At least Delilah made life more interesting, I'll give her that.

Sessions with Wilcox ground on.

"Dr. Wilcox, I really *do* love my mother," I said one morning, a couple of weeks after our argument. "Can you love someone and hate them at the same time?"

"Not at the same moment—but you can fight with someone you love, Leslie."

"But when I tried to, she walked out on me!" I said.

"Yeah, so?" she said casually, taking a long drag on her cigarette. "You're still here, aren't you?"

"Well . . ." I hesitated. "But I fixed it."

"My dear, I guarantee you, you'd be here anyway."

No, said the dictator. She's lying. Trying to con you, make you give in. "I lost two more pounds," I told her.

"And the price of gold went up. We were talking about your mother."

"Which Gold," I said, smiling slyly. "What're you trying to do, give me more guilt?"

"You're playing games, Leslie. Is that how you want to spend the rest of your life?"

My life? I thought. That's really funny—being that it's neither living nor mine. No. No, Leslie, it isn't funny.

142

It isn't funny at all. You can be quick and clever, but Wilcox is right—you're running away.

"How can I have a life if I don't exist?" I said. It's OK, Leslie—*Wilcox* doesn't know Leslie-never-cries. "Dr. Wilcox, I swear, I swear that's what it feels like—don't you believe me?"

"Leslie," she said almost tenderly. "Of course, I believe that's what you feel—I can only try to imagine what it must be like. But there *is* a person inside you who got angry at Mom—"

"Yes, and I paid for it," I said acidly. "I lost two pounds." That wasn't me talking, I thought. That was the dictator. The dictator-me. Me? I bit my lip.

Yes, Wilcox; I'm not stupid. A little crazy, maybe —well, OK, a *lot* crazy—but not stupid. I see the chains, I do—I can follow them link by link, but somehow I keep winding up in the same place. In the bathroom throwing up or in front of my lunch tray saying no.

"See where I always end up?" I said.

"It doesn't have to be that way."

"Dr. Wilcox, I didn't *choose* to get sick!"

"No, not consciously, but you're hanging onto it now, aren't you?"

"I don't *want* to want to. But I want to. Can't you do anything to make me *not* want to want to?" I said in desperation. What a jumble!

"If you want to get well badly enough, you can," she said.

Like flying? Is it like that? If I wish hard enough, if only I want to badly enough, will I really be able to fly? I want to fly far away, to never-never land, where I'm not ashamed, where it's OK to eat all sorts of things, not a humiliating, dirty thing to do. I'd be beautiful and free, and there'd be no scales, no mirrors. Never-be-hungry land, never-be-judged land, never-be-Mom land, always-be-me land. Second star to the right, and straight on till morning—is that how you get there? Oh, how lovely to fly! Think lovely thoughts! Ice cream, candy—no, no, Hiller, this will never do, I scolded myself in mock anger. Schmaltz, pure and simple. Wilcox is right —it's not the food; it can't be. But how come the minute I eat, all that nice logic falls away?

"Leslie, why don't you try eating, just as an experiment?" Dr. Wilcox said. "Just to see for yourself how much better you'll feel."

"Up here?" I said, pointing at my head.

"You'll just feel better. Trust me."

I squinted at her.

"Look, you can always go back—" She held out her hands, palms up. "You know how to do it."

"Oh, *please*, Miller," I begged, and Carrie and Nicole clasped their hands, jumping around like puppies. "*Please*, we won't tell—please take us for one itty-bitty walk in the garden?"

She gave in. Jessica was gone on a one-day pass, her parents having picked her up at eleven, picnic basket in hand. She was up to ninety-two pounds—at her height, she's not far from being OK, at least on the outside, I thought. It was a gorgeous May Saturday, and the floor was fairly quiet, as it always was on weekends. We filed into the elevator and went down to the first floor. Miller led us down a corridor, left, past the vending machines, through the chapel, and outside into the sun.

"Wow," I said, feeling almost giddy. We scampered down the walkway, Miller thumping after us, saying, "Hey, no running! Come on!"

"Wow," I said again. Nicole and Carrie were grinning ear to ear, and I threw my head back. The sky was a dazzling sapphire blue. I had never noticed how beautiful it was, not the way I did then. And the moon was out! To the moon and back, Mom, do you love me to the moon and back? You know what? Right this very second, I don't really care.

We sidestepped off the path, and I took off my zoris. "Hey, you guys, come on," I said, as Carrie pulled off her fuzzy pink slippers. Nicole stepped out of hers gingerly, leaning over to pick them up. The grass was cool and soft against my feet; there were dandelions splattered all over the lawn and flowers coming up on the far side in neat little rows.

"You look like Julie Andrews in *The Sound of Music*," I said to Nicole, who had spread her arms out eagle fashion and thrown her head back as I had. "Well, *half* of Julie Andrews," I added.

"It's so beautiful, isn't it?" Carrie said. People were sprawled on the grass, eating lunch or just talking: nurses; a few patients here and there; men who were

145

probably interns but weren't wearing their white coats so you couldn't tell.

"OK, kids, time to go back," Miss Miller announced.

"*Already?*" we whined, like a bunch of kids wanting to stay up just-five-more-minutes.

"Don't push your luck, tootsie pie," she said to me. "They'd have my head if they knew I brought you out here."

That evening I went to make my daily phone call and began dialing my home number. I stopped in the middle, bit my nail, and pushed down the lever to get my dime back. I dropped it back into the slot and re-dialed.

"Hello?" a voice answered.

"Hi, is Cavett there?"

"Hold on. Cavett!" the voice shrieked, dropping the receiver. "It's for you!"

Finally she came. "Hello?"

"Cavett?"

"*Leslie?*"

"Yeah."

"Leslie, hey, where are you? Are you home?" she sputtered.

"No, I'm still up here," I said.

"I thought you weren't allowed to call! I mean you're not, are you?"

"Hey," I said jauntily. "You know me and rules. Aren't you glad?"

"Sure I am, are you kidding?" There was an awkward

146

silence, and then she said, "So listen, I mean, how are you?"

"I'm—um—OK, I guess. I mean, I'm fine. I guess." I laughed weakly.

"Do you think they'll let you come home soon?"

"I don't know. I haven't exactly gained weight, exactly," I said. "But I guess I'll have to if I ever want to get out of here."

"Yeah," she said. "Oh, Leslie, guess what? I saw Avram at a dance last week."

"You're kidding. Did he grow?"

"I think he shrank, actually," she said, laughing.

"We're a perfect couple then." Leslie, you're not so bad sometimes. Really, you're not.

"Hey, Les," Cavett said. "I don't mean to sound like everyone else, but—can't you eat just a little so you can get out of there? I mean, I don't care what you look like or anything, but can't you just get healthy enough to come home?"

"Maybe," I said hesitantly. After all, I can always go back to it, like Wilcox said—I know how to do it.

"Do you think you'll be out by the middle of June?"

"I don't know, maybe—"

"Dad's doing a movie out in L.A., and we're going with him for a month," she said. "But we're not leaving till June twentieth. Oh—listen, I want to ask you something." She paused significantly. "My hair is nearly down to my shoulders. Should I cut it, or let it grow?"

I began to laugh then, a lovely, happy laugh.

147

"Leslie?" she said, sounding scared.

"Try it long," I said, wiping my eyes. "You can always cut it, right?"

"Yeah—I'll wait till you can see it anyway. Shit," she said half to herself. "Why should you care whether or not I cut my hair, for Christ's sake? You're in a hospital, and—"

"But, Cavett, I *do* care," I said. "I always cared. I try not to care about things, but I can't help it." She was silent. I looked out the glass door and saw Delilah pacing up and down like a caged tiger, working off her tomato juice while she waited for the phone. "I better go, someone else wants the phone," I said.

"OK. Hey—thanks for calling," she said. "I've really missed you a lot."

"I've missed you, too." It was a white lie; I hadn't thought about her that often since I got there. But if I had, I realized, I would have missed her. "Maybe I'll see you before you leave."

"OK, Leslie. Hey, just tell me one thing—are they helping you?"

"They're trying to," I said finally.

"Well . . . that's something."

"Yeah. Look, I'll see you. OK?"

"Sure, OK. Bye, Les."

Click.

Nikki used to tell me she couldn't understand why I was anorexic; after all, I was talented, while she "couldn't do anything." Translation, from ano-pig-latin:

I was a worthwhile person, she wasn't. I knew that had nothing to do with it; I tried to explain it to her, but I don't think she ever really listened. I guess we all had a gift for not listening. Nobody listened to any of us, but we ate up everyone else's words till there was such a din inside we couldn't hear anything anymore.

For one thing, I'd tell Nikki, I couldn't tell who I did things for, me or Mom. Dad, too, but mostly Mom. Even if I started out doing something because I wanted to, she loved it so much I kind of lost track of it. Sort of like when an electric train switches from one track to another. Next thing I knew, my track was empty. "But what if they hated everything you did? You wouldn't like that either," Nikki would say. I know what she meant, but I think for me it would have been easier. It's having the contrast. I don't know why I need it more than some other people, why I turned out the way I did: Mom? Dad? My second-grade teacher? Liza, Roger, the books I've read, movies I've seen, who knows how many banana peels, and maybe something I was just plain born with. Parents can't really win no matter what they do.

For another thing, I'd tell Nikki, if people ate on the basis of how much talent they thought they had, you couldn't get hold of cottage cheese for love or money. I mean, who isn't insecure in some way or other? You don't take care of yourself because of talent or anything else. You just—you just do it *because*. Like Delilah; only she had it all topsy-turvy, like the rest of us.

Wilcox used to say, "You want to be taken care of," and she was right. But I also don't. I want to be a skeleton—but I also want to be attractive. I want to die—but I also want to live. I don't deserve to feel good—but oh, I want to so much! Being stingy is fun, Mom? Isn't it just! But it's mean, too, isn't it, Mom? Mean to yourself, and mean to all the people around you whose guilt you eat up like candy. I bet you're not happy being this way. No more than I am. Maybe you think you're the rat in that film, too. I don't know. Maybe someday you'll play the game and I won't play with you. I love you, Mom. And you love me. But it just isn't that simple.

T. S. Eliot said, "You cannot face it steadily, but this thing is sure, That time is no healer: the patient is no longer here." Well, I'm still here, for a while anyway, but he was right. Perhaps when people talk about time healing wounds, what they really mean is distance, and time doesn't always give you that.

Maybe I've told you things and wasn't listening to myself; maybe if I listen again, I'll hear something different. Not anything rational, because that never helps —something in my heart, telling me who the dictator really is, and setting me free.

There are so many places I've dreamed of going to, real places, I mean—and I'd like to learn to play that mazurka myself, to see if I could make it dance, too. I'd like to read that Emily Dickinson poem and be able to hear what Cavett heard. I'd like to meet Avram in Roger's body, and I'd like to taste lobster—would you believe I've never tasted lobster, ever?

I used to want to have myself all figured out, like a

mathematical equation, but I'd probably hate being able to reduce myself to that—just as much as I'd hate being graded for it. Let's see: Leslie + Margolee + Hiller - ? . . . Well, it's not winning that counts; it's how you don't play the game, right? I think, at this point, I'd give myself a C+. And if anyone asked me, right this second, whether I'd go to the right or to the left, I'd say—to the right. And straight on till morning.

HEY, DOLLFACE
Deborah Hautzig

How do you separate loving as a friend and sexual love – or do they cross over sometimes? Val Hoffman knows that there is nothing wrong, or bad, in the way she feels about Chloe. They are friends, and their friendship has a trust and intimacy which is special for both of them. But sometimes outsiders, even family, can misjudge and label such friendships and labels are frightening because they distort the truth. In this perceptive, funny and wholly convincing novel about two teenage girls, young, unsure, and on the brink of sexual awakening, Deborah Hautzig charts that all-important time between adolescence and adulthood – that fragile moment when we first begin to learn about loving other people.

'This excellently constructed book is an honest documentary of the tribulations of becoming an adult. It is a sharp, credible and moving book.' *Learn*

THE FOX IN WINTER
John Branfield

When Fran's mother, a district nurse in Cornwall, first took her down to Penhallow Farm to help on a visit to old Tom Treloar and his wife, Fran had no idea how close she would become to this old man, his home and his past. While Fran's visits fast become the most important event in old Tom's day, he opens up new interests and pastimes for her, and when he tells her about the seal cave, Fran decides to enlist the help of fellow sixth-former Dave in a search for the old carved fox-and-geese pieces that Tom Treloar had found and left behind so long ago.

In John Branfield's sympathetic hands the positive and life-enhancing aspects of a relationship between young and old are convincingly portrayed.

'The story is a love story, of a teenage girl's awakening to awareness of adult emotions . . . The contrast between the stark reality of the hospital world and the wild beauty of a hidden Cornish valley is yet another delight in this book which excels at so many levels.'   *British Book News*

'Easily John Branfield's best to date . . . It's admirable honesty makes it both touching and amusing.'   *Books for Keeps*

It's My Life

ROBERT LEESON

'You're playing hard to get,' Sharon had said as Jan walked off, away from school and from Peter Carey's invitation to the college disco on Friday night. Was she? Jan didn't really know. She wanted time to think things out, ask Mum what she thought.

But when Mum doesn't come home, Jan finds her own problems taking second place, as she is expected to cope with running the house for her father and younger brother Kevin, as well as studying for exams and trying to sort out her feelings towards Peter. Slowly she realises what sort of life her mother led, the loneliness and the pressures she faced, and with this realisation comes Jan's firm resolve that despite the expectations of family, neighbours and friends, she will decide things for herself; after all, 'It's my life.'